DANGEROUS PAWS

CORRINE WINTERS

Join my newsletter by clicking here!

ONE

Ember skidded through the grass, staining her palms green and releasing a fragrant scent. She wondered if the smell of grass would forever be associated with tragedy.

Ember lifted her gaze, mouth agape with horror as the painted, ceramic urn flipped through the humid Louisiana air. Her husband's memories lay trapped inside, sealed by a magic spell. When the urn shattered, the memories would be released to the ether—lost forever.

Cedric stood too far away to stop the flying urn. Ash mouthed the words to a spell, a valiant effort Ember knew doomed to fail. No one could cast swiftly enough to stop the urn from shattering on the ground.

A golden-furred flash sped past Ember and dove under the urn. Kali! Her familiar darted under the urn just as it was to hit the ground. Ember cringed when Kali cried out in pain. The urn fell over onto the grass, unbroken—for now. Kali walked a few paces away, shook her back leg vigorously, and then stood protectively over the urn.

Cedric pulled his service pistol and aimed at the man

responsible for knocking Ember off her feet—Jimmy Hoffa, recently returned from a long exile in another dimension. His mouth gaped open, and the point of his barrel drifted toward the ground.

Ember turned to look at Hoffa and her mouth gaped in horror. Gone was the middle-aged man she'd exposed as a murderer in Driftwood. In his place stood a being so aged its flesh seemed to melt off its bent, bowed bones. Jimmy Hoffa's eyes took on a rheumy cast, his suit draped over his skeletal form like a tent.

"What's happening to him?" Ember asked in horror.

"Ha! He's aging all those decades in a matter of minutes," Munkilok said, using April's mouth. "Looks good on ya, sucker!"

Ember knew Hoffa was not a good man. He was a killer, a fact she had uncovered personally. Yet, she couldn't stand to see him suffer. She looked away until Hoffa collapsed, face first, his internal organs failing in rapid succession.

"Well, that solves the mystery of Jimmy Hoffa," Cedric said with a chuckle. "Too bad we can't tell anyone."

"No one would believe us anyway." Ember looked over to Ash. "I suppose we should give him a proper burial?"

"Let him rot in the sun," Munkilok said eagerly.

"How long has it been since April has been in control of her own body, Imp?" Ash glared at April.

"Hey, there was dimensional travel, and a guy aging into a mummy. It's a bit much for a first grader, so I took the wheel. If you humans were better at taking care of your younglings, she wouldn't need me in the first place, you know."

"I'm doing the best I can," Ember snapped. "You're not helping. You're hindering."

"You just don't like me, witch."

Ember sneered. "You're right about that much. I guess we agree on one thing."

"Touché." April bowed and then ran into the house. Ember wasn't sure who was in control of her body at that moment. It was just another one of her mounting problems.

Ember turned to Ash and nodded. They stepped on either side of Hoffa's body and linked hands over him. They chanted a spell in the witch tongue, asking the earth to take Hoffa's body back to nature.

Tendrils of root shot up and wrapped around the skeletal corpse. The earth seemed amorphous as a sponge, bubbling up around his body as if it were sinking. Bit by bit, Hoffa disappeared into the ground.

A purple flower sprang up in the middle of his new grave. Ember and Ash parted. Ember stared down at the flower and sighed.

"May he find a better path in his next life."

"Here's hoping." Ash picked up the urn carefully and cocked an eyebrow at Ember. "First things first. I say we load this puppy up with spells to keep it safe."

"Like a barrier spell so it won't break?"

"To start, sure. We should also ward against incorporeal entities, oh, and use a dimensional anchor charm to keep anyone from teleporting it away from us."

Ember nodded. "A tracking spell, too."

Cedric looked between the two of them and then rubbed the bridge of his nose. "We just got back from a magical dimension with flying dragons and lightning storms. Can we give the magic a rest for a bit, please? I could use some normalcy."

"Speaking of normalcy," Ash said. "Shouldn't we be opening the Pub soon?"

Ember looked at the time and cursed. Her hand flew in front of her mouth and Cedric chuckled.

"Been hanging out with sailors?"

Ember turned to Ash. "We'll put a few wards on the urn, then head into the pub. We can snag a couple of grimoires to read if it slows down after lunch."

"Sounds good to me." Ash turned to Cedric. "Can you drop April off at school while we take care of the Pub? We're running late."

"Certainly." Cedric looked at Ember for a long moment, then suddenly came forward and embraced her.

"Cedric?" Ember patted his arm, unsure of what to do. It felt good to feel her amnesiac husband's arms around her again after so long, but his manner upset her. "What's wrong?"

"You have a habit of putting yourself in peril," he said, holding her tight. "I just want you to...just be careful, okay?"

Cedric released her, and turned to trot toward the house. "April, or Munkilok, or whoever is in there, get your book bag. Time for school."

Ash carried the urn toward the house, Ember falling behind. She took one last look at the purple flower waving in the morning breeze, and then put the case of D.B. Cooper's murder behind her for good—figuratively and literally.

TWO

Ember and Ash hustled to keep up with the flow of customers coming into the Broken Broom Pub. It seemed her elevated bar food favorites had been greatly missed during the days she took off to settle April in.

The town's Doctor, Dennis Dalton, sat at a table with his wife, Sharon, and son, Mark. They smiled happily as Ember stopped by their table bearing a heavily-laden tray.

"Who had the T-bone and eggs?"

"That would be me, Miss Ember," Mark said.

"Look at you, Mark. It seems like not that long ago you were just a little thing, now you're taller than your father." Ember laid the plate in front of him while his mother frowned.

"Mark, dear, she's a married woman. You no longer call her Miss. It's Mrs. Jamison now."

"Actually, it's Ember McNair-Jamison," Ember replied with a smile "but Mark can call me Ember if he wants. I don't mind."

"Stop fussing, Sharon, can't you see Ember's busy?"

Dalton gestured to his plate. "I had the oatmeal and grapefruit with a side of hash brown."

"Oats and grapefruit and hash," Ember said, laying his plate down. "And you must have had the BLT?"

"Yes, thank you."

As Ember rushed away from their table to help Ash in the kitchen, she heard something which made her cringe. Doctor Dalton called one of his friends and said;

"The Pub's open again. Yes, it's even Ember cooking today. Oh, it's not that busy."

Ember rushed into the kitchen and turned off a deep fryer, pulling onion rings out of the grease. She gave the baskets a good shake and trotted to Ash's side to help her plate biscuits and gravy.

"It's crazy busy this morning," Ash blinked sweat out of her eyes and glanced over at Ember. "Is it a holiday or something?"

"Not that I know of. It's about to get worse, too. Doc Dalton just invited all his golf buddies over for brunch."

"At least they're good tippers. This is murder, Ember. If we weren't using magic we'd never keep up with this crowd."

"I know. My small-town Pub has become all too popular of late. Maybe I should sell it?"

"Sell it?" Ash was aghast. "Sell the Broom? Are you even being serious right now?"

Ember sighed. "I don't know. I used to love the Broom. Now, though, it seems like a burden. I don't know. Let's just survive this breakfast rush and prepare for the inevitable lunch deluge."

The bell rang at the entrance. Ember hurried back to the lobby, arms laden with three orders of biscuits and gravy. She smiled at the new entrant, glad to see it was only one customer.

"Hello, Hanky-Bob," she said to the tall, shaggy, bearded man in grease-stained overalls standing in the doorway.

"Morning, Ember. You're open for business, right?"

"Sure am," she said with a smile. "Come on in."

Hanky-Bob pushed the door open fully. He called over his shoulder. "You were right, she is open. C'mon."

Six men filed in after Hanky-Bob. Ember felt her heart sink. She and Ash had their work cut out for them today.

Gradually the breakfast rush slowed, allowing Ember and Ash to catch up. Ember paused by a prep table where Kali lay stretched out, eyes barely open.

"Are you all right, Kali?"

"I'm fine. Just a little sore where the Urn hit me."

Ember frowned. She felt Kali's back and discovered a tender bump. "You poor thing. Let me put some healing unguent on you."

"That stuff smells! My prey will scent me coming a mile away."

"You know I don't like you killing so many birds anyway, Kali. Hold still and let me put it on you."

The obstinate cat endured, making a great pathetic show of herself. Ember darted back out into the lobby, wiping her hands on a stained rag as she went.

She paused, face dropping into a frown. Most of the patrons remaining in her lobby clustered around Hanky-Bob's table. The shaggy mechanic held court with a story which held everyone's rapt attention.

"Well, that's what I heard, anyway," Hanky-Bob said to Doctor Dalton.

"Incredible. I wonder what this means for the community?" Dalton shook his head.

"What's going on?" Ember asked.

"It's Mayor Stubbs."

"Oh no, is he ill?" Ember asked.

"No, but he is retiring," Hanky-Bob said.

"Oh my." Ember pursed her lips. "He's been Mayor for a long time. Almost as long as I can remember."

"Yeah, nobody's bothered to run against him in at least four elections now. If he's retiring, that leaves the field wide open."

"Who's going to be our next mayor?" Mark asked.

"Maybe you should run, dear," Sharon said to Doctor Dalton.

"Are you kidding? Who wants to do a bunch of tedious paperwork on top of what I already do with my practice, not to mention I'm already the town's medical examiner. It would be a conflict of interest."

"Oh, poo, you could do both."

"Hey," said a red-bearded man sitting with Hanky-Bob's party. "You know who would make a great mayor? Ron Olberman."

Most of the lobby rolled their eyes, cried out in dismay, or started cursing.

"Are you kidding? That jerk has been trying to buy the town out from under us for years, and you want to hand him the keys to the city?" Hanky-Bob scowled at the red-bearded man. "How can you even support a con man like him?"

"Hey, I think he could make Caucherie into a big town," the red-bearded man snapped back. "What's wrong with progress?."

"You're talking out your behind, Ramsey," Hanky-Bob said.

"Why don't you try looking at it from somewhere besides your point of view?" Ramsey taunted.

"Why don't you try shutting up?"

"Why don't you make me?"

Hanky-Bob rose from his chair, knocking it flat behind him. Ember stepped between the two would-be combatants and pushed them back.

"Hey, not in my bar. You want to roll around like a couple of high school pubescents, do it outside."

Hanky-Bob looked abashed, his face flushing red. "I'm sorry, Ember."

He picked up his chair while Ramsey stood up and threw money on the table.

"You just wait and see. Olberman will turn Caucherie around. This town could use some energy."

Ember sighed as she watched him leave. Ron Olberman as mayor?

She hoped Stubbs' retirement was just a rumor, or more trouble would be visiting the sleepy Louisiana town soon.

THREE

Ash plopped down on a stool and blew out an exasperated sigh. "That was a heck of a breakfast rush. The town's growing, Ember. We really should think about hiring some help—unless you were serious about selling the tavern."

"I don't know if I was or not, honestly." Ember packed Cedric's lunch of tavern leftovers. She placed a thick buttermilk biscuit on top of a collection of scrambled eggs, sausage, and cheese and sealed it in a Tupperware container. "Hiring some help may not be a bad idea, but..."

"But what?" Kali asked, perking up from where she licked her paw.

"But...Caucherie has always been charming because it's so small. Sure, we get tourist foot traffic, but not too much. Just the right amount to keep us living comfortably. Now that Olberman's developing so much, the town is changing. I'm not sure I like that."

"Did you think we were going to stay a sleepy little town forever?" Ash shrugged as she swirled the ice around in her tea glass.

"Kind of, yes." Ember shot a frank look over at Ash. "This town has witches, shifters, and other strangeness just as a matter of course. The only reason it hasn't caused more chaos is because the town is so small. If the population explodes, I've got a feeling something bad could happen."

"Bad?" Ash cocked an eyebrow. "You mean like murders, memory-stealing demons, and trips to parallel dimensions?"

"Good point." Ember headed for the door. "I'll be back to help with the lunch rush, I promise. I just want to run this to Cedric."

"You'd better," Ash said with a half-smile.

Ember drove to the sheriff's station, her mind occupied with thoughts of progress. Hanky-Bob may have been more vitriolic than Ember would have liked, but she could understand his anger and resentment for Olberman.

She pushed open the glass door to the station and found Cedric preparing to leave.

"What's wrong?" Ember asked.

"There's a mess at City Hall. It seems half the town is trying to register as a mayoral candidate all at once, and it's getting ugly."

"I'm coming with you," she said. "You can at least eat your biscuit on the way."

Cedric perked up. "You made biscuits?"

He nibbled on bites of the fluffy biscuit as they drove the short distance to City Hall. Ember frowned at the sight of the town square filled with people. Most of them seemed anxious and agitated. She could feel an energy in the air akin to a brewing thunderstorm.

"What's going on?" Cedric asked Doctor Dalton as they strode up to the edge of the milling throng.

Dalton squinted in the bright Louisiana sunlight as he

turned to face Cedric. "There's not enough Mayoral candidacy application forms to go around. Reverend Carmichael is bringing the bingo tumbler from church to create some sort of lottery, but a lot of folks think it should be first come, first serve."

"I don't understand, why can't they just print out more applications?" Ember asked.

"In order to be official, they have to come from the Louisiana Lieutenant Governor's office. More are on the way, but they won't be here until next week."

"Swell." Cedric looked around at the crowd, which grew increasingly volatile. "Looks like it's not just people here to register themselves."

Ember followed his gaze and saw quite a few signs supporting Olberman.

"For heaven's sake, why?" she sighed.

Hanky-Bob grimaced, a look of pure hate boiling in his normally laconic gaze. "Olberman has brought a lot of jobs to the area, like as not. He's changed some folks' lives for the better, sure. Too bad he takes a dump on the rest of us while he's at it."

"It's getting ugly," Cedric said.

Ember groaned when a black limousine pulled up at the edge of the town square. "It's about to get uglier. Speak of the Devil, and he appears."

Cedric and Ember exchanged glances. She knew they thought the same thing; If Olberman ran for mayor, he'd probably win. That would change the little town's dynamics forever.

As Olberman exited his limo and the crowd caught sight of him, it grew increasingly wild. His supporters cheered at the top of their lungs like exuberant Saints fans during a touchdown, while his detractors reacted with vocal derision.

"Oh boy," Cedric said. "I'm going to get on my radio, call in some Staties to bolster security."

Ember chewed her lip anxiously. She knew the nearest state trooper station was a good twenty minutes away. What if the powder keg exploded before then?

Olberman approached, escorted by a twenty-something woman with blonde hair and brown eyebrows, and a man whose polished veneer and good looks seemed too good to be true. So much so, Ember considered casting a spell to detect glamours in play.

"Mr. Olberman," Cedric said with strained politeness. "I'm not sure this is a good time for you to visit City Hall."

"It's the perfect time," Olberman said, his greasy used-car salesman smile in place. "I heard the Mayoral race in Caucherie is wide open."

"Not to you, it's not," Hanky-Bob said, bearded face twisted in a sneer. "You have to be a Caucherie resident to qualify."

"Oh, I think you should check the qualification guidelines again, Mr. um, Bob. It only states one must be a resident by the time one takes the oath of office."

Olberman chuckled and gestured at the young man behind him. "But not to worry. I'm not here to register for candidacy. Caucherie's a great town, but it's impractical for me to live here. My son-in-law Earl will be registering."

"So you can have a puppet in office?" Hanky-Bob said, eyes narrowed to slits.

"I'm no one's puppet, sir," Earl said, stepping forward and shaking the confused and off-balance Hanky-Bob's hand. "What's your name, good sir?"

"Uh, Hanky-Bob," he said.

"Oh, yes, I've heard a lot about you. Your auto-body shop has quite the reputation for quality. You're just the type of constituent who I intend to serve, one with roots strongly set in the Caucherie community. What would you say if I got you a subsidy for your business, say fifty grand as a lowball estimate?"

"You can't bribe voters," Ember frowned.

"I'm not bribing anyone, I'm laying out my small business initiative, and explaining how it will benefit my constituents personally." Earl turned to face her. "Ember McNair-Jamison, right? You run the pub here in town."

"That's right," Ember said cautiously.

This guy's got a silver tongue if I've ever heard one.

"I can assure you, Ma'am, that you will benefit from the subsidy yourself. Wouldn't you like to do some renovations on your pub? I'd imagine there's some maintenance that you could catch up on as well."

"Well, my parking lot is cracked—hey, wait a minute. You can't dangle money in front of people and expect them to just fall in line. Not all of us is a greedy industrialist."

"I'm just trying to make the government work for the people instead of against the people," Earl said.

A loud shout and a crash caught everyone's attention. The bingo tumbler had arrived, only to be knocked over by the press of humanity rushing up to take part. Reverend Carmichael lay on the sidewalk, eyes wide with horror as the crowd threatened to trample him.

"Oh no," Cedric said. "The State Troopers didn't get here in time. It's about to be a riot."

FOUR

Ember's gaze snapped all over the mob scene as she considered her options. A barrier spell to protect the Reverend? No, that would reveal her secret to the entire town. A charm spell? Those only worked on one person at a time.

Then she had it. Ember muttered the spell under her breath, channeling the abundant natural eldritch energy found in the swamp through her body. A warm pulse throbbed through her body as the skies overhead darkened with gathering storm clouds.

The skies opened up in a torrential downpour. No warning drizzle, no clap of thunder. Just a sudden deluge so strong it cooled the hottest passions and made all run for cover.

"Good work, Ember," Cedric said, rain running down the brim of his hat. "I fear it's only a temporary fix, though."

They helped the Reverend to his feet and salvaged the bingo tumbler ball. Cedric stepped in front of City Hall and spoke to the few souls brave enough to remain in the rain.

"Everybody go home. Nobody's getting an application today."

"You can't do that," shouted Ramsey. "We're exercising our Constitutional rights."

"I'm with the local yokel," said a man sheltering under the awning, Ember's eyes widened, because she couldn't believe what she saw.

"Kevin Whitman?" she gasped. "But—you're supposed to be dead."

The thin-faced man's eyes narrowed. "Kevin Whitman is dead. I'm his brother, Chad. He left his compound to me in his will."

"Nice to meet you," Ember said, feeling abashed. "I'm sorry. You just look a lot like him. Your brother wasn't a bad man, he just harbored a lot of paranoia."

"Paranoia? You mean he'd awakened to the people running our lives through media manipulation and psychoactive drugs in the water supply. If you want to call that paranoia, I suppose that's your interpretation."

Ember cursed herself silently. Again, she'd put her foot in her mouth.

"Speaking of interpretation, one could say that Olberman is responsible for my brother's death."

"He wasn't, though. It was a local thug named Krebs—"

"Kevin got poisoned at Olberman's town hall meeting, at Olberman's buffet, by people Olberman hired. You sure he's not to blame?"

Ember had no answer, but Cedric came to the rescue.

"Everybody go home," Cedric said, a firm edge crawling into his tone. "As Sheriff, I absolutely have the right to shut down City Hall to protect the public welfare, and that's just what I'm doing. We'll try this again tomorrow in a more orderly fashion."

He turned to Ember and spoke lower. "And the State Troopers are here to provide additional security."

Ember returned to the tavern in time to help Ash with the lunch rush. Ash cocked an eyebrow at Ember as she hastily donned an apron.

"Sunny skies, then it opens up like Noah's Flood? Was that your doing?"

"Yes," Ember said. "I thought it would be better than a riot."

"Well, it's affecting business. Not too many folks coming in the door today."

"After the breakfast rush, I'm not going to complain."

Ember glanced at the spell book and sighed. "So much for reading it in our spare time."

CHANNELING magic on a scale grand enough to affect the weather left Ember exhausted. Cedric took care of dinner and April's homework, much to her relief. She took a bath and turned in before nine pm. Not only was she tired, going to bed earlier than Cedric avoided a lot of awkwardness. Though they were married, to Cedric's perspective they'd known each other only for a little over a month.

Her last thoughts before drifting off to sleep were of finding a way to reunite Cedric with his memories.

Ember's eyes opened in the morning sunlight. Something lingered in the air, like a low guitar chord reverberating after the strings had been plucked. She wasn't sure how she knew, but something had happened in the night. Something bad.

Cedric stood in the bathroom, shaving in the steam-streaked mirror. She sighed, thinking of how they used to shower together. Now Cedric did so by himself. It wasn't fair, being a new bride with a husband who didn't remember any of their relationship.

She padded downstairs and checked on April, then started coffee. Ember decided it would be a cold cereal kind of morning, though she made sure to peel and cut a few apples to shore up the breakfast.

Ember walked April out to the school bus, then returned to find Cedric on the phone.

"...try and keep this quiet for as long as you can. I want to get a look at the scene before the media descends like a pack of locusts."

Cedric looked up at Ember and ended the call. He opened his mouth to speak, but she cut him off.

"Someone's dead aren't they?"

Cedric nodded. "Your, uh, witch sense tell you that?"

Ember pursed her lips and sighed. "I'm not sure. I had a feeling something bad had happened last night. Cedric, I'm not sure this body being found is the end of it. I think it's only the beginning."

"We don't even know if there's foul play involved," Cedric said with a shrug.

"I know, we don't want to compromise the investigation with personal bias or self-fulfilling prophecies but trust me. This time, there was foul play."

They drove out to the town softball diamond. Deputy Smothers stood beside a polished dark blue BMW, dusting for prints. He waved as they pulled into the gravel lot.

"What's the good word, Smothers?" Cedric asked.

"I found a ton of prints, but of course we don't know who all they belong to yet. One of them could be our killer."

"If it's a murder, Smothers. Don't jump to conclusions."

Smothers scoffed, spreading his arms out wide. "Sheriff,

come on…this guy turns up dead the day after almost causing a riot downtown? It's got to be someone who got mad and killed him, don't you think?"

"I assume nothing. As law enforcement, our job is to follow the evidence." Cedric gestured at the car. "When you finish those prints, run them back to the office straight away. Log into the FBI database and see if we get any hits."

"You got it, Sheriff."

Ember and Cedric walked onto the grassy field, donning vinyl gloves as they went. She felt a jolt of pathos when she spotted Olberman's body laying across the field. A breeze sighed through the trees as birds chirped merrily in their branches. It was entirely too pastoral a scene for a dead body.

"No obvious wounds," Cedric said, carefully moving around the body and inspecting it thoroughly with his gaze. "We'll have to look at his front half to be sure, though."

Cedric snapped photos of the body and the surrounding area. Ember narrowed her gaze as she considered Olberman's placement. She stood at his head and looked back across the field.

"What's wrong?" Cedric asked.

"Look at how the grass has been smashed flat," she said. "I think somebody dragged our victim's body after he was dead."

They walked the trail of flattened grass out past the foul line. Cedric snapped more pictures and knelt down in the grass.

"No sign of a struggle. If he was murdered, Olberman never saw it coming."

"Someone he trusted? Or at least wasn't afraid of?"

Cedric frowned. "Maybe. We'll have to let Dalton take a look to be sure."

"How's he settling into the new job?"

"Pretty well, I reckon. Hasn't had much to do, of course, but that's a good thing, right?"

Ember nodded. "It's a good thing all right, but he'll be busy today, I'm afraid. Who would want to kill Olberman?"

Cedric let out a short, derisive bark of laughter. "Who wouldn't? We've got a suspect list a mile long, and that's just the people here in Caucherie. A man like Olberman makes a lot of enemies on his way to the top."

Ember stared down at Olberman's still, seemingly-unmarked, corpse. His face seemed drawn in pain rather than repose.

She hoped his expression wasn't a harbinger of things to come.

FIVE

"I say we start with Chad Whitman," Cedric said as they awaited the county coroner's arrival.

Ember frowned thoughtfully. "He did seem to blame Olberman for his brother's death."

"Besides being kind of a nut job just like Kevin." Cedric sighed. "I know it's bad Karma, but I was looking forward to a Whitman-free existence. Now there's another one. How many brothers does he have?"

"Hopefully just the one." Ember spotted the Coroner's van turning the last corner before the softball diamond. "Whitman's not our only suspect, of course, but I have to admit I like him for this."

They spoke with the Coroner briefly before climbing into the squad car. Ember called Ash and worked out a schedule where Sage would help with the breakfast shift, and Kathy would assist Ash with lunch.

"You know, Kathy's the smart one. She doesn't actually work in her Café, she just manages it."

"Yeah, well, I started the Pub more because I liked

talking to people and drinking rather than trying to be a tycoon, okay?"

Ash chuckled. "I'm just saying. There are options beyond selling the Pub. Good luck with Whitman."

"Thanks."

Cedric glanced over her as they headed out of town toward Whitman's fenced compound. "Did you guys get it all worked out?"

"Yeah, it's fine. Sage and Kathy are going to pitch in."

They turned onto the gravel road leading to Chad Whitman's property. To her surprise, Whitman was out and visible, standing beside his fence and accepting a pizza delivery.

"Oh great," Whitman said as he took the stack of boxes through the security slot in his gate. "I knew, as soon as I heard the news this morning, that you'd be at my doorstep."

Cedric cocked an eyebrow as he strode up to the fence. The pizza delivery man looked nervously at the Sheriff and took a half step back.

"Now, what did you hear on the news?"

"Are you kidding? Ron Olberman is dead. I knew, with what I said yesterday, and the way that law enforcement persecutes my family, that you'd show up here and accuse me of killing him."

"Excuse me," the pizza delivery man said in a breaking voice. "I need to collect payment."

"Right." Whitman sneered as he dug out three twenty dollar bills from his wallet. He handed it and three pennies to the driver. "See? Cash is king, despite what you might think about morality, law, or order. Men like Olberman buy their own justice. Well, he can't do that anymore, can he?"

"You seem awfully happy he's dead," Cedric remarked.

He cocked an eyebrow at the three pizza boxes in his arms. "Also pretty hungry."

"Oh, are you the pizza police now? Going to regulate how much gluten and dairy I can have in my diet? And you're darn right I'm happy that the world-elite charlatan is dead. That's not a crime, unless they've struck down the first amendment."

Cedric pursed his lips. "Mind if I come in and take a look around?"

"Yes, I mind!" Whitman glared defiantly at them through the fence. "I know my rights, Sheriff. Show me a warrant first before I let you onto my sovereign property."

Cedric laughed. "Have it your way, Mr. Whitman. I hate to break it to you, but you're a person of interest in this case, so don't leave the county. Is that clear?"

"I'm going inside to call my lawyer right this second. Is that clear?" Whitman took his pizzas and stormed off, dogs barking somewhere in the distance. "Quiet, you mangy mutts. None of this is for you."

Ember and Cedric climbed back into the squad car and exchanged glances.

"That went well," she said.

"Should have figured he'd stonewall us." Cedric's eyes narrowed to slits. "How did word get out so fast? I wonder if Smothers ran his mouth."

"I doubt he'd call the press."

"No, but there's a lot of folks he might tell who might. Let's go back to the station and see if Mr. Chad Whitman has a criminal record."

They drove to the station, both of them silent and deep in thought. Ember thought of Olberman's body, and the way it had been dragged. What had been the point of that? And how, exactly, did he die?

"I wonder if Doctor Dalton's found out anything yet," Ember said.

"Give him a bit. He had appointments today, and it won't be until later this afternoon he's even available."

Ember nodded, silently fuming at the delay. She couldn't blame Dalton for honoring his scheduled appointments, but she wanted to know more. The case pulsed in her head, a problem which demanded solving.

She had to admit, the thrill she got while pursuing a lead or investigating a hunch far outstripped the fun she had at the Pub any longer. Perhaps Ash was right. Maybe it was time to look into stepping back from the day-to-day operations of the Broom.

They returned to the station and sipped on coffee while Smothers ran Chad Whitman's criminal records. "There's not much here. Arrested for disturbing the peace at a couple of political rallies."

Ember pointed at the screen. "See here? He was charged with sending a threatening letter to the Governor's office. Charges were dropped when he underwent anger management counseling."

"I'd say he's, at the very least, an aggressive man," Cedric said. "There's no history of violent crimes, though. He could just be a very obnoxious, big-time talker."

"Maybe." Ember frowned, pointing at the screen. "How come there's nothing in his record before this point?"

"His juvenile records are sealed." Cedric stroked his chin. "It'll be a nightmare trying to get them unsealed, too."

"For the time being, we don't have anything solid to link him to the crime, even if he does have a motive." Ember stared at Whitman's face and frowned.

I'm not done with you yet, Chad. Not by a long shot.

SIX

Steam rose from the cups of tea in Ember's hands as she stepped up to the living room sofa. Ash looked up from where the grimoire lay spread on the glass coffee table and accepted one of the cups. Kali lifted her head off Ash's lap, yawned, and stretched.

"What, no tea for me?" Kali griped.

"You were asleep," Ash replied.

"I'm a cat, duh. I sleep fourteen hours a day. That doesn't mean I don't want tea when it gets brewed."

"I'm sorry, Kali," Ember said, reaching out to stroke her familiar's fur. Kali flinched when Ember's fingers slid over her spine. "Does your back still hurt?"

"No," Kali said stiffly. "I'm fine. Let's crack this case."

Kali studiously stared at the grimoire. Ember frowned, realizing Kali was still yet to fully recover from having a heavy urn drop on her back.

Ember resolved to let Kali rest as much as possible until she recovered.

"Hey, what do you think about this one?" Ash tapped the open book. "It's called *Nystul's Dodder-Begone.*"

Ember rested her bottom on the sofa and set her tea aside to cool. She pored over the grimoire and frowned. "I'm afraid not, Ash."

"It's a spell about restoring memories."

"Restoring memories in a person with dementia, and, even then, it's only temporary." Ember shook her head. "I wish it would work, but it won't."

April thumped into the living room, jumping with her legs held together. She jumped all around the sofa and coffee table in a wide circuit, creating a great racket and causing the pictures to rattle on the walls.

"April, why don't you go play outside," Ash suggested.

"I don't want to." April stopped and looked at the cup beside Ember. "Will you make me Tea, Miss Ember?"

"You can have mine, sweetie," Ember replied, barely glancing away from the tome. "You know, Ash, this is a unique situation. It's going to take a unique spell."

Ash stiffened up. "Ember, no."

"Did you put honey in this?" April asked, staring at the cup in her hands with distaste.

"Yes I did."

"I don't like it with honey. Can you make me some different tea?"

Ember sighed. "April, sweetie, we're in the middle of something very important. I'll make you tea later."

April pouted. "I want tea now."

"April, go play outside," Ash said harshly. April's face contorted into a contemptuous sneer.

"*You* go play outside," Munkilok said. He grabbed Ash's tea off the table and poured it out on the floor. "There, now nobody gets tea. I hope you're happy."

"Munkilok, you little—" Ash went to give chase, but Ember grabbed her arm.

"Let it go, sis."

"But he just—"

"I know, I saw him. I was right here, you know. There's not much we can do."

"We can exorcise his annoying little butt."

"I'm afraid April will see that as a betrayal. She's lost her mother and father, so she probably feels like everyone will leave her. What we need to do is convince Munkilok to leave of his own accord."

Ash snorted as they used paper towels to clean up the spill. "Well, at least you didn't suggest we write a custom spell for him. How do we convince him to leave, then?"

"He's not your usual possessing entity. Munkilok actually thinks he's helping April, protecting her. We have to convince him that April is going to be okay, and he'll probably depart."

"Probably?"

"Best we can do, under the circumstances. If he doesn't leave on his own, we can talk about more drastic means, but I at least want to try using honey before we break out the vinegar."

"Fair enough." Ash looked outside the living room's bay window and sighed. "Here comes Cedric, and we have to tell him we've made no progress."

"We made progress. We know we need a custom spell."

Ash slapped a hand over her face and heaved an exasperated sigh. "Are you out of your mind? We could wind up turning ourselves into toads, or stone statues. Or tear a hole through to a Hell dimension. There's a reason spell books exist, sis. They're the proven commodities, the magic that is time-tested and known to function the way it's supposed to."

Ember cocked an eyebrow. "What about Throckdwaddle's Full Sail Chaos Polymorphic Escape?"

"Special case, and I never learned that one, anyway."

"Really? I could teach you—"

Cedric entered the front door, smiling warmly at them as he walked across the living room floor. His eyes darted to the open spellbook and he cleared his throat. "So, any progress?"

Ember sighed. "Not yet. We do have a theory about how to proceed though."

"Really? How?"

"It's just a theory at this point, Ash interjected. "So, what's up? You look antsy, Cedric."

Ember glanced over at Ash. She'd deliberately drawn the conversation away from the custom spellcrafting.

"Doc Dalton has just performed his first official medical examination of a potential murder victim, and he'd like us both to be there in person to go over his findings."

"Great, I'll get my purse." Ember glanced over at Ash. "We'll talk more about this later."

Ash nodded, looking none too thrilled with the prospect.

"I'm coming, too," Kali said.

"Kali..." Ember sighed. "Maybe you should sit this one out? You're still in a lot of pain, even with the healing herbs we've given you."

"I'm tougher than a two-dollar steak," Kali said stubbornly.

"You realize that's not a compliment, right?" Ash said drolly.

"Um..." Ember rifled through several ideas on how to keep her familiar safely at home. "Ash could really use your help, though, Kali. Isn't that right Ash?"

"What? Why would I--ow!"

Ash rubbed her bicep where Ember had punched her, realization dawning in her eyes.

"I mean, yes, absolutely I could use Kali's help."

"Well, if she needs my help," Kali said. Ember believed the feline was more relieved than she let on.

"We'll be back later. Keep me posted if you find anything."

"Will do," Ash replied.

Cedric drove them into town, his face dropping into a frown when they reached his small Sheriff's station. "What's all this, now?"

"Oh no," Ember sighed. "We should have expected this, with Olberman's fame and celebrity status. It's the press corps."

"I'm not good with making official statements," Cedric said anxiously.

"You'll do fine." She kissed him on the cheek, and he flinched. "Oh, I'm sorry."

"It's fine," he said swiftly, smiling ear to ear. "It's totally fine. I guess I can just say 'no comment', right?"

"That's the spirit."

Cedric honked his horn, attempting to get the media to part enough he could get his squad car in the parking lot. They didn't seem to notice, or, if they did, they ignored him.

"Dang it," Cedric muttered. He hit his cherries and siren for just a moment, and the startled reporters parted like the Red Sea before Moses. "Don't they realize this is a busy office?"

"They're just doing their jobs, Cedric."

"They can do them just fine across the street," he muttered. "Here goes nothing."

A perky blonde shoved a microphone in Cedric's face, her blue eyes glazed with a predatory gleam.

"Sheriff Jamison, is it true Olberman was murdered?"

"I have no comment at this time," Cedric said, pushing the microphone away gently and moving toward the building. Another reporter rushed up and attempted to obstruct his path.

"Sheriff, is it true that you allow your civilian wife to accompany you on investigations? Isn't that highly irregular?"

Cedric glared at the man until he shrank back. "Again, I have no comment at this time."

The blonde moved up beside them again, undaunted from his earlier brush off. "Sheriff, is it true that Chad Whitman is a person of interest in this case?"

Cedric flinched. "Who told you that?"

The blonde smiled. "I have my sources. Kathy Kent, New Orleans Sun-Times. Maybe we can talk later?"

"I'm a happily married man," Cedric said, rejecting her business card. "But thanks anyway."

"Don't you want to know how I knew about Whitman?"

Cedric stared at her with a narrowed gaze until she smiled. "If you change your mind, call the Sun-Times office and ask for my extension."

"I won't."

Ember still reeled from what Cedric had said. Happily Married...had he really meant that, or was it just a way to brush Kent off?

"This is ludicrous," Cedric said. "They're like a pack of rabid animals."

Ember nodded as they entered the safety of the station house at last. "I concur, but getting rid of them might involve giving them what they want. You should schedule a press conference or something, then maybe they won't hound you so much."

"Maybe. Not my cup of tea, but I suppose I could." Cedric gestured toward the rear exit of the station. "Let's go see if, maybe, by some miracle, Olberman died of natural causes and this will all end here."

"Yes, let's hope so." Ember replied.

"You really think it will happen?"

Ember laughed. "Nope."

SEVEN

Cedric and Ember walked around the back of the sheriff's station. There, a smaller, plain concrete structure housed the new town morgue. Its capacity remained around a dozen, which seemed excessive to Ember. At least, she hoped it was excessive.

They pushed their way inside. Ember shivered, and Cedric directed her to the public-use jackets hanging near the entrance.

"No thanks," she said, the tip of her nose growing cold.

"I know they're not the most fashionable—"

"It's not that. Those jackets hang in a place designated to contain dead bodies. The taint of death is on them, in an Eldritch sense, and I'm trying to limit my exposure to dark forces these days."

"Fair enough," Cedric replied, cocking his eyebrow. Ember could see him visibly tamping down his curiosity. They had other fish to fry, as it were.

They pushed open a set of double doors and entered an examination chamber where Doc Dalton stood beside

Olberman's body. Stitches on Olberman's chest indicated the recent autopsy.

"So, how did Olberman die, Doc?" Cedric asked.

Dalton gestured at Olberman. "Cardiac arrest."

"So, natural causes?" Ember asked.

"I didn't say that." Dalton showed them photos he had taken during the autopsy. Ember looked away in disgust, but Cedric moved in for a closer look.

"See those black craters on the surface of his liver, Sheriff?"

"I do. What does that indicate? Some sort of cancer?"

"No, those are burns to his internal organs."

"Burns? But he doesn't have a mark on him."

"Not true. Here's a photo of the victim's back, near the L5 vertebrae. See those two small holes? My theory is those are the contact points of an electrical-based weapon, like a taser. Someone inundated Olberman with so much electricity, it caused his organs to sear like a grilling steak."

Cedric looked at Ember and cocked an eyebrow. She knew what he wanted and performed a minor spell to check for the presence of magic about the body.

She gave Cedric a subtle shake of her head. Whatever killed Olberman was mundane and not magical. In a way, she was relieved. Though that didn't make Olberman any less dead, or catch the killer in their midst.

Cedric turned back to Doctor Dalton. "Were there any other injuries on our victim, Doc?"

"Some abrasions from being dragged through the grass, or maybe when he fell after being electrocuted." Doc Dalton shrugged. "All postmortem, in any event. As far as I can tell there was no fight or struggle prior to his demise. He did bite off the tip of his own tongue while being electrocuted, but that's not uncommon."

Ember looked at Olberman's face, which seemed contorted in a miserable, restless grimace.

"How long did it take?" she asked in a soft voice.

"How long did what take?" Doc Dalton asked.

"Olberman. How long did it take for him to, um, expire from the cardiac arrest?"

Doc Dalton swallowed and tugged at his collar. "I can't be entirely certain, of course, but judging by the fact Olberman had time to chew through his own tongue...I'd say at least two or three minutes."

"Two or three minutes?" Cedric asked, his jaw dropping open.

"Two or three minutes of indescribable agony for the victim," Doc Dalton added. "During which time they could do nothing but convulse and suffer. Olberman likely knew he was dying, he just couldn't do anything about it."

Cedric wiped a hand across his mouth. "Do you think this could have been an accident, Doc? Like maybe, I don't know, someone wanted to kidnap Olberman and hold him for ransom? He was a rich guy."

"Not a chance, Sheriff." Doc Dalton's eyes grew clouded with troubles. "The entire time he would have deployed the device, it would have been obvious they were killing him. The smell of burnt flesh, smoke coming out of Olberman's nostrils and mouth...it wouldn't have been pretty, or an accident."

Cedric sighed. "Thanks Doc. I wish you had better news for us."

"I live to serve," Dalton replied with an exaggerated bow.

Ember and Cedric strode from the cold chamber, digesting what they'd just learned. Ember suppressed a shiver. Cedric glanced over at her and cocked his eyebrow.

"What's wrong?"

"It's just the thought of someone standing there for three minutes, slowly cooking a man from the inside out."

Cedric nodded. "Yup. We're either dealing with a perpetrator who had an extreme grudge against Olberman, or..."

"Or what?" Ember asked.

Cedric shook his head, as if he didn't want to believe the words about to come out of his own mouth.

"Or, we have a perp who stood there and watched Olberman fry because he enjoyed the show."

Ember couldn't repress her shudder the second time. "Let's hope it's the first one."

"Agreed." Cedric patted his belly. "Is there a possibility of a quick bite at your Pub?"

Ember nodded. "I should check in and see how it's going, anyway."

She cast a glance back at the morgue as they strode away. Somehow, the idea of a mundane torturing a person to death was far more chilling than even facing off against a demon. She really hoped it was just a crime of passion and not something worse.

Desperately.

EIGHT

"Here we go, again," Cedric said, staring at the mob of press and onlookers outside of the Sheriff's office. They had yet to mob him, but Ember knew it was coming. Cedric's eyes fell on a man selling hot dogs and lemonade to the gathered press corps and their camera crews. "Son of a gun, are you kidding me?"

He walked over to the balding man behind the folding-table stand and glared down at him. "John Gruberman, are you seriously profiting off my misery?"

"Hey, it's a capitalist world. Ron Olberman taught us that before he passed on to the great beyond. You've got to be ready when opportunity knocks."

"Hey, it's the Sheriff, he's back!"

Cedric rolled his eyes. "Kill me now."

Ember took his hand and squeezed it. "Just keep saying 'no comment,' no matter what they ask you. We just have to make it to the car."

"True enough."

The press corps lived up to their name, pressing in on

them. Kelly led the charge, asking awkward questions designed to get a rise out of Cedric.

"Don't you think the public deserves to know if they're in danger?" she asked.

"No comment," Cedric replied, shutting his door firmly in her face. He started up the squad car and backed up swiftly. The press darted out of range, like minnows fleeing a shark.

"Thank goodness we're leaving them behind," Ember said.

"Don't speak too soon." Cedric looked grimly in the rearview mirror. Ember turned to glance over her shoulder and groaned in exasperation. The press were piling in their cars and following them.

"Cedric, as a private business owner, I have the right, by Louisiana law, to refuse service to anyone or no one as I see fit, right?"

"That's right, you do."

"Then those annoying remora won't be allowed to set foot inside of the Pub."

"Hmm. What if they want an order of onion rings and a brew?"

Ember chuckled. "They can come in then, but as soon as they start asking questions or taking pictures, I'm giving them the boot."

They drove to her tavern, a few short blocks away. Ember wondered if the gaggle of press following them were a portent of the future in Caucherie. Would the small town she'd loved forever turn into something she couldn't recognize? Was progress really inevitable?

She came to no conclusions on her musings before they reached the pub. Ember paused at the entrance while

Cedric went inside. As the press gathered on the sidewalk, she crossed her arms and laid down the law.

"Listen up," she snapped, scaring some of the press corps. "And listen good. My husband is here for a much-needed lunch break. Anyone who asks him a single question, or me, for that matter, gets the boot right back out the door. Now, if you want some buffalo wings or a light beer, please, by all means come inside."

She entered the tavern before they had a chance to respond. No one followed her inside, which Ember counted as a victory.

Ember found Cedric ensconced in his favorite booth, near the kitchen entrance so he and Ember could chat as she darted in and out serving guests. He hadn't sat there in some time, not since he'd lost his memory.

"We've got a hungry Sheriff," Kathy said, coming out of the kitchen and smiling at Cedric. "How have you been?"

"I've been well, thank you," Cedric replied. "Yourself?"

"Can't complain. I've stepped back from running the café, I just count the beans now. Have you met my daughter, Willow?"

A thin-boned young woman came out to shyly stand beside Kathy. Kali stretched out in her arms, seeming in utter bliss. Ember smiled and joined the conversation.

"Willow, you've gotten so tall. I remember when you were knee high to a grasshopper."

Willow smiled nervously, showing off braces-clad teeth. Kathy gestured to Willow. "Go ahead, ask the man for his order."

"S-sorry. What would you like, Sheriff?"

"Oh, whatever's laying around, it doesn't have to be too fancy."

Kathy turned to her daughter. "Go make him a Rueben. You remember how?"

Willow nodded and headed back to the kitchen. Ember called after her. "Willow, dear, could you make that two?"

"Sure thing, Miss Ember."

"Oh, for heaven's sake, call me Ember. It's fine."

Willow smiled and disappeared from sight. Ember settled in next to Cedric while Kathy went to help her daughter in the kitchen.

"Can you think of any type of weapon which might have done that to Olberman?" she asked.

"Let's do a little web surfing and find out."

Cedric used his phone to search for different electrical-based, self-defense devices. As they scrolled through, Ember sat beside Cedric in the booth, scrunched up beside him. Cedric didn't flinch when she leaned her body against his.

"Could it be one of those things, the stun guns?"

Cedric squinted at the screen. "Maybe, but I doubt it. Our perp would have had to stick it in and hold it there while Olberman convulsed for three minutes. I'd say we're looking at one of these."

He scrolled down the images on the screen until they reached the image of a yellow and black taser gun. "See, this model launches two sharpened leads, which stick in the victim's skin. Then electrical current passes through twin wires into the leads."

"So the leads would stay put, even if Olberman convulsed about." Ember nodded. "It looks like the same distance between leads, too. But how can we be sure?"

"We order one, that's how. Good thing I'm in law enforcement and can hurdle the usual background check."

Cedric tapped on his screen. "Done. Overnight delivery from New Orleans."

The bell over Ember's door rang. She turned toward the tavern entrance, worried she would see a member of the press corps. A strange man a few years older than Cedric strode into the tavern, doffing dark sunglasses and placing them in his pocket.

He spotted Cedric and moved swiftly to their table. "Sheriff, I've got some questions for you."

"Hey, buddy," Ember scowled. "Didn't you hear me before? No press in here, unless it's to eat."

The man cocked an eyebrow. "My name's not buddy."

He dug out a badge and showed it to Ember. "Agent Robert Ulysses Reddy, Federal Bureau of Investigation, at your service."

NINE

Cedric gasped. He squirmed out of the booth and stood before the FBI agent.

"R.U. Reddy, is that you! You old son of a gun, how the devil have you been?"

"I can't complain, how about yourself, Slick Ric? Everything still hanging all right?"

Ember cocked an eyebrow. "Slick Ric?"

"Just a nickname," Cedric said. "R.U., let me introduce my wife, Ember. Ember, this is an old friend of mine from our days in the state patrol, R.U. Reddy."

"You can call me R.U., Ma'am," Reddy said with a smile, politely shaking her hand. "Sorry about the confusion. I was just trying to sneak up on my old buddy Slick Ric here."

Ember chuckled. "It's fine. No harm done. Are you hungry?"

Reddy frowned. "I am a bit peckish..."

"Say no more," Ember said. "I'll get you a sandwich going. Would you like something to drink?"

"Got sweet tea?"

"Naturally."

"Then I'd love some of that, thank you." Reddy turned to Cedric and punched him in the arm. "Ric, you sly dog, you got yourself a gorgeous wife. No wonder you keep her to yourself."

Ember fought to keep a scowl off her face. She didn't want to cause friction between Cedric and his friend, but something about Agent Reddy rubbed her the wrong way.

"Man, that Reddy guy loves the sound of his own voice, doesn't he?" Kali quipped.

"Be a nice kitty," Ember said. "He's Cedric's friend."

"I was being nice. I could have said he has diarrhea of the mouth."

Ember rolled her eyes as they entered the kitchen.

She arranged for a third sandwich and returned to the lobby to find Reddy and Cedric howling with laughter.

"And that's when the third chick came stumbling out, nothing on from the waist down, and smacked Jimmy with the fly swatter, right!" Reddy leaned on Cedric to support himself, so great was his mirth.

"I'd forgotten all about that," Cedric replied.

"That's because you were drinking tequila and licking salt off that one chick's neck—what was her name? Melinda or something like that?"

"Missy," Cedric said, snapping his fingers.

Ember cleared her throat and placed the three plates on the table. Cedric and Reddy sat down at the booth, still chatting like mad.

She knew it wasn't Cedric's fault, but the fact he could recall all of R.U. Reddy's stories—not to mention the name of a woman he hadn't known for years—but not any of their life together rankled.

Ember tried to stow her feelings deep down, where they

wouldn't be on display, but Cedric and Reddy kept inadvertently pushing her buttons.

"What ever happened to you and Krista Collins?" Reddy asked with eager eyes.

"Oh, Krista," Cedric said, his face breaking into a wide, wistful grin. "I'll tell you what, I never met a girl who..."

He glanced over at Ember, then cleared his throat. "Yeah, I remember her, I think. Vaguely."

Ember bit into her sandwich, the crunch of the toasted rye bread making it so she couldn't hear Reddy's annoying banter with Cedric. She vowed to herself she would survive this awkward lunch without driving a wedge between Cedric and his old friend, but it was hard.

"Listen," Reddy said, dabbing his mouth with a napkin. "I could sit here and swap stories all day and all night, but that's not why I'm here."

Cedric's smile faded, his blue eyes growing hard. "All right, let's deal with the elephant in the room."

"What elephant would that be?" Reddy asked, brows climbing high on his face.

"You're here to take over the case from me, aren't you?"

Reddy held his hands up and made a downward gesture. "Now, let's tamp down that kind of talk. I'm here to observe and assist, not to take over, I swear."

Cedric cocked an eyebrow. "The Governor and I have an understanding. He tends to keep his finger out of the Caucherie pie, if you catch my meaning."

Reddy took a long drink of iced tea and wiped his mouth with the back of his hand. "I know you and the governor are pretty tight. Gives you a ton of leeway, and, to be fair, you nearly always get your man, don't you?"

Cedric smiled. "Thanks to Ember, yes."

Reddy frowned at Ember but continued on as if Cedric

hadn't spoken. "Thing is, Ron Olberman's a pretty big deal. He might be an even bigger deal in death than he is in life. The Justice Department is just...concerned that the investigation into his death could turn into another OJ Simpson debacle. I mean, you've seen the press."

"Yeah, and felt them, too. They nearly crushed us to death in the parking lot." Cedric grinned. "Well, if I have to have an FBI agent dogging my every step and second guessing my every move, I'm glad it's you, Reddy."

"Hey, I'm serious about not stepping on your toes, Slick Ric. Dead serious." Reddy grinned. "Now, let's talk shop. What did your ME have to say?"

Ember answered before Cedric could. "It looks like a homicide, most likely intentional and premeditated."

"Is that so?" Reddy said, a touch of condescension creeping into his tone. "Do tell."

"Uh," Cedric said as Reddy and Ember glared at each other "it looks like our murder weapon is likely to be one of these stun gun devices. I've already ordered one over the internet, and it'll be here tomorrow."

"Good thinking," Reddy said. "Even if it's not the same model the killer used, it'll get us in the ballpark range. Who do you like for this?"

"Who don't I like?" Cedric laughed. "The man had his enemies."

"There's got to be someone you have in mind, though."

Cedric nodded. "Yes, a man named Chad Whitman. His brother died recently—"

"I know all about Whitman. You're barking up the wrong tree." Reddy waved dismissively.

"What makes you say that?"

"Simple. Whitman got himself on an FBI watch list for

sending threatening letters to elected officials. He's all talk, no action."

Reddy went to take a drink of his tea and found it empty. He looked to Ember and held the glass out to her. "Could I get a refill, sweetness?"

Ember smiled her way through a burst of anger. "Sure."

She took the glass and walked stiffly through the kitchen entrance. Ember hoped they would solve the case swiftly and be done with Reddy.

Otherwise, she was going to give serious consideration to turning him into a toad.

TEN

Ember and Cedric drove from the tavern in silence. He glanced over at her, noting her icy demeanor, and opened his mouth, then closed it.

They passed beneath the boughs of trees whose branches arched over the road to entwine like lover's fingers. Clumps of Spanish Moss hung from many of the trees, creating a dense canopy which shaded the road ahead.

Cedric again made as if to speak. Ember turned sharply toward him and glared. He heaved a sigh and spoke at last.

"Is something the matter?"

"No, why would anything be the matter?" Ember stared out the window.

"Because you're sulking."

"How is my sulking your problem?"

"Uh...did I do something to make you upset?"

"No, nothing at all...except maybe letting your buddy R.U. Reddy talk to me like a servant."

"I—I mean, I didn't...I was just...we haven't seen each other in a long time, and—"

"Save it. I don't want to hear your excuses."

"I'm sorry I didn't step in and stick up for you, Ember. Really."

Ember, taken aback by his seemingly heartfelt apology, felt a lot of her bluster drain away. "Thank you."

"No problem." Cedric turned his gaze back to the road, apparently thinking the matter was over just because he'd apologized.

"It is kind of a slap in the face that you remember some floozy's name but not all the dates we had at the botanical gardens."

"That's not my fault," Cedric said. "But what the hey, I'll apologize for it anyway. In fact, why don't I just apologize for everything that goes wrong in your life?"

"You don't have to yell," Ember snapped.

"I'm not—" Cedric cut himself off and spoke in a lower tone. "I'm not yelling. I'm venting."

Kali put her furry paws on the center console and looked up at Cedric.

"You were pretty close to yelling, Cedric."

Cedric's lips thinned into a tight line. "If I was, then I'm sorry."

Ember sighed, rubbing the bridge of her nose as they passed beneath the trees. "Look, I'm sorry. It's not your fault, the amnesia I mean. You didn't ask for it."

"You didn't either." Cedric cleared his throat. "Uh, any progress on that front?"

Ember shook her head. "Not yet. There doesn't seem to be a spell written that can do what we need to do."

"Oh." Cedric sighed. "So, getting the urn with my memories back was pointless."

Ember turned a sharp glance his way. Cedric seemed bitter and hurt by the prospect.

"No, it wasn't." Ember reached out and put her hand on his powerful shoulder. "It wasn't pointless."

"You said there's no magic way to fix it."

"No, I didn't. You need to listen to the actual words I say instead of assuming you know what's going on. I said, specifically, that there was no spell *written* that would help. That doesn't mean Ash and I can't write one of our own."

Cedric cocked an eyebrow incredulously. "You can do that?"

"Of course, we can. Where do you think spells come from in the first place? Someone has to write them. It's just a terribly arduous process..."

Ember's voice trailed off. Cedric prompted her when she lapsed into silence.

"What aren't you telling me?"

Ember glanced at him sharply, then settled back in her seat and sighed. "It's not an entirely...safe...process to write and cast a unique spell. There are risks."

Cedric frowned. "I don't like the idea of you putting yourself in danger for me."

"I'm willing to take the risk. Ash and I working together have a good shot at making it work."

Cedric's knuckles grew white on the steering wheel. Ember still had her hand on his shoulder, and she felt the way he trembled with tension.

"Cedric, what's wrong?"

"What happens if..." he swallowed hard. "What happens if you can't restore my memories? Ever? What happens then? Do I...do I have to move out?"

"Move out?" Ember shook her head. "No! I mean... you're a grown man capable of making your own decisions, but...moving out seems kind of drastic."

Cedric lapsed into silence. Ember couldn't make out

what he was thinking for the inscrutable cast to his handsome features. When she could no longer endure it, she spoke again.

"Cedric...do you want to move out?"

He snapped a shocked gaze her way.

"It's understandable," Ember said, her voice breaking a little. "I mean, according to your memory, you're a swinging bachelor. Why would you settle down with a stranger?"

"Ember," Cedric said. "I don't want to move out."

She reacted as if slapped. Her throat grew tight, and she struggled to swallow.

"Oh." Ember sniffled. "Okay."

Kali rubbed her face against Cedric's elbow and purred. "That was the right thing to say."

They passed out of the trees and merged with the highway. Ember groaned when she saw two men covering up a Skoal Tobacco billboard with one promoting Earl Kleen for Mayor.

"And so, it begins," Ember muttered.

Cedric pursed his lips, his brow furrowed in thought as he stared at the billboard image of Kleen. "How much do you think Kleen stands to inherit from Olberman's death?"

"Um, well, I'm not his accountant, but I imagine a lot. I mean, it might go to his wife and not him, but I can't imagine that meek little mouse of a housefrau not letting Kleen run the companies."

"So, we're talking billions of dollars, then." Cedric did a careful U-turn on the highway.

"What are you doing?"

"We're heading over to Mr. Kleen's new house, being as he's a resident and all. I'd like to ask him a few questions as to his whereabouts on the night of his father's disappearance and murder."

"He's just going to lawyer up," Ember cautioned.

"Maybe, maybe not. If we're careful and don't spook him, make it seem like we're on his side trying to find out who harmed his father—"

"I get it. He might be more forthcoming."

Cedric cocked an eyebrow. "Or would you rather go home and do it tomorrow?"

"No," Ember said. "Let's go talk to Kleen. Like as not, he's looking like our best suspect."

Unless her hunch was right, and Olberman's killing had nothing to do with money but was done for the sheer glee of slaughter.

ELEVEN

Ember whistled as they pulled onto the private drive and she got her first look at Kleen's manor house.

"Wow. Look at that porch, Cedric. Haven't we always wanted a wraparound porch like that?"

"Uh, I think so," Cedric replied. Ember cursed herself silently. Of course, Cedric didn't remember any such thing. "Looks like the lights are on. Car's out front."

Cedric pulled into the circle drive before the manor house proper. As they exited the squad car, a woman in simple black and white servant's garb appeared out of the front door and walked onto the porch.

"I'm sorry, but this is a private residence," she said with an unaffected air of snobbery and a Yankee accent which made it clear she was not a local.

"Sheriff's department, Ma'am," he said, tapping his badge. "But I have a feeling you knew that already. Is Earl Kleen available? I need to talk to him."

"Mr. Kleen is busy in his study," the woman said stiffly.

Cedric put one hand on his hip and laughed. He looked over at Ember and smiled, as if to say 'isn't she precious?'

"Well, now, I suppose I could leave—"

"Perhaps that will be for the best—"

"—and return tomorrow with a warrant for his arrest."

The maid blanched. "A warrant?"

"Yes, you know what those are, right?" Cedric gestured at the house and grinned. "Mr. Kleen is a person of interest in the murder of Ron Olberman, his father-in-law. If he won't talk to me willingly, I can only assume it's because he has something to hide. Now, in light of this, are you sure you don't want to get Mr. Kleen for a little chat?"

The maid sighed and turned to enter the house. A few minutes later Kleen stormed onto the porch, his veneer of schmaltzy charm rubbed away clean.

"You've got some nerve, coming to my house and threatening to arrest me. I have committed no crime."

Cedric put his hands on his hips and looked Kleen square in the eye. "I never make threats, Mr. Kleen. I just need to talk to you, and we can do it the easy way or the hard way, but it's going to happen."

Kleen shook his head and rolled his eyes. "Heaven save me from these yokel Keystone Cops. All right, you want to talk. So, talk."

"You told me earlier your father-in-law had come over for dinner. What time did he leave?"

"I told you, around ten," Kleen said.

"Ten? You said nine the other day."

Kleen's face grew dark. "Nine, ten, what does it matter? Why are you trying to pressure me? I had nothing to do with Ron's death. He's been nothing but kind to me."

"Yeah, I can tell you're real broken up about it," Ember

said. "Putting up your campaign posters a day after your father was found dead."

Kleen straightened up, assuming his stage persona of a great statesman. "I feel like I owe it to my dearly departed father-in-law to win the Mayoral race. It's what he would have wanted."

"Yeah, your bleeding heart's staining your clothes," Ember muttered.

"Mr. Kleen, are you sure you can't remember anything else? Something that Olberman may have said before he left? Like his destination, or people he thought to meet?"

"No," Kleen snapped. "Now, I've answered your questions. Get off my property, and if you come back with a warrant I'll have you know the legal department of Olberman Corporation has a larger annual budget than your entire county."

Kleen went back into his house and slammed the door. Ember and Cedric faced each other and laughed without much mirth.

"Not so charming when there aren't television cameras around," Ember said.

"No joke. Come on, let's go home."

LATER THAT NIGHT, Ember sat on the edge of the bed, fighting the tangles in her hair with a silver brush. Her hair reached her waist, and took a lot of maintenance. Cedric used to brush it for her, before he'd lost his memory.

Ember's belly roiled with frustration. Cedric's memories remained locked away from him, even if they'd been found. April's possessing entity was no closer to leaving, and they'd stalled out on the murder case.

And, now, she couldn't even manage her own hair. It was enough to make her scream in frustration.

Ember started when Cedric entered the room. Her eyes took in the hard knots of muscle on his abdomen, the rippling curves of his pecs. He hadn't walked around without a shirt much since losing his memory.

Cedric noted her struggles with the brush. He settled onto the bed behind her and took the brush from her hand.

"It's all right," she said. "You don't have to..."

She sighed when Cedric carefully ran the brush through her hair, starting at the top and working his way down with efficient, neat strokes. It was as if he'd never forgotten.

"I'm a lot better at this than I expected," Cedric mumbled as he took a long strand of her hair on his palm and used the brush to gently remove tangles.

"Muscle memory, maybe. The Glawkus' attack isn't all that well understood."

Cedric grunted. He settled into his task, his knees pressed up against Ember's bottom as he worked the tangles free from her hair. Her hair slowly took on a shiny, ordered appearance once again.

"Your hair is so beautiful, Ember," Cedric whispered as he stroked his fingers through her long locks. "And so soft..."

His hands swept onto her shoulders. Ember gasped, stiffening up at the unexpected touch. Cedric slid his hands down her arms, taking the shoulder straps of her top with them as they went.

Ember shivered as he exposed her naked body by increments. His arms encircled her waist. Ember clutched at his forearm, not to pry it away, but to hold on as if for dear life.

"Cedric..." she moaned.

"Shhh," he kissed her bare neck, lips gentler than an alighting butterfly. "I want you, Ember."

She turned about into his fiery embrace, their lips pressed together in a deep kiss. The soft cries that filled the night had nothing to do with pain or fear, until they fell asleep in each other's arms.

TWELVE

Ember awoke to the delightful aroma of coffee wafting into her nostrils. She yawned and stretched, sore in all the right ways, a wide smile crossing her face. Kali lifted her head from the pillow next to Ember and yawned widely.

She stumbled into the bathroom to the unmistakable sound of bacon sizzling on a cast iron skillet. Ember sighed as she squeezed toothpaste onto her brush. She loved the way Cedric made bacon; cut into small strips and fried in a bit of butter.

The stairs creaked as she headed down to the kitchen. She cast a smile at Cedric. He stood before the skillet with his phone awkwardly propped between shoulder and chin while he took scrambled eggs off the stove. By the time her bare feet touched the cool kitchen tile, he'd scooped the eggs into a large serving bowl with stylized chickens prancing about in effigy.

Ember settled in beside April, wondering if it were her or Munkilok she'd be dealing with that morning. "Good morning, April."

"Morning, Miss Ember." April's food sat largely uneaten. She toyed with a gel bracelet on her wrist instead.

"That's a cute bracelet. Where did you get it?"

"My friend Krista gave it to me," April said. "She has a lot, but she only gives them to people who are her special friends. I'm her special friend."

"That's great." Ember gestured at the plate. "Why don't you try taking one more bite of everything before you go and brush your teeth?"

"Okay." April scooped the bacon into her mouth like a St. Bernard who hadn't eaten in three weeks. Ember's eyes widened as the girl shoveled the remains of her plate down her gullet in rapid succession."

Cedric came over and placed the bowl of steaming scrambled eggs on the table. Ember put her hand on his forearm and rubbed, smiling up into his face. Cedric didn't smile back. He seemed almost panicked, in her estimation. He disengaged and moved to the other side of the table to seat himself.

Maybe he's acting like this because April's here?

She decided to let it go for the time being. Last night had been the first time they'd made love since Cedric's amnesia. It had to be messing with his head.

Ember's heart broke a little. It seemed they'd not reached the turning point she'd hoped for. She resolved to treasure the memory of her previous night in case it didn't happen again for a while.

They ate their breakfast in silence, Cedric busy with his phone, Ember going through a grimoire on spell creation. When April was seen out the door to the school bus, she set her book down heavily and sighed.

"Do you regret what happened last night?"

Cedric was so startled he dropped his phone. He hastily scrambled to pick it up off the floor, face turning red.

"I—no. No, I don't regret it."

"Then why are you acting like I have leprosy when I touch you?"

Cedric heaved a sigh and fixed her with a pained gaze.

"I don't know. It's...it was like my body could remember you, but my mind couldn't. I keep thinking it should just come back to me, and it won't, and I'm mad as a hornet about it."

Ember reached out and took his hand across the table. "We can get through this, like we've gotten through everything else."

"I hope so." Cedric slipped his hand free of her own and fixed her with a somber gaze. "I wanted to wait until you finished your breakfast and coffee before telling you. Another body has been found."

Ember gasped. "Who?"

"Yet to be determined. Smothers is out there holding down the fort until we get there."

"Where?"

"Out by Hanky-Bob's place. Might even be on his property line, I don't know."

"The body is at Hanky-Bob's place?" Ember's belly did flip flops. "It's not him, is it?"

"I'm pretty sure Smothers would have told me if it were Hanky Bob."

Ember dug her phone out of her purse. "I'll call Ash and tell her she's on her own this morning. She's going to kill me."

Ash picked up on the second ring. By way of greeting, she said "No."

"No?"

"No, I'm not opening the tavern by myself again."

"There's a body—"

"There's always a body! It's too much work for one person, and I can't handle it."

"All right, all right. I'll call Kathy and see if Willow's available."

Ash groaned. "She's so slow!"

"She's learning."

"I'm sorry, but when God was handing out brains, Willow thought he said trains and said 'no thanks, I'll take the next one'. No wonder she can't even get into junior college."

"Ashley!" Ember gasped. "That was mean."

Ash sighed. "You're right, it was. I'm sorry."

"Kathy told me Willow's a very slow, deliberate learner. But once she gets something down, she's got it down. Please be patient with her."

"All right, but you owe me for this."

Ember chuckled. "Ben and Jerry's or Hagen Das?"

"Better be both."

Ember met Cedric's querying gaze. "Everything all right?"

"It will be. I've been thinking of stepping back from the day-to-day at the Tavern. Maybe just turning it over to Ash to run, I don't know."

"You love the Broom, though."

"I did love the Broom, but I have a family now, and so many other things going on..." Ember sighed. "I don't know. I have to think about it some more."

They drove out to the edge of town, to a heavily wooded area where Hanky-Bob made his home. Cedric parked next to Smothers' patrol car. They strode through ankle-high grass toward where Smothers stood in the shade of a willow tree, looking down at a shape in the grass.

"I smell death..." Kali hissed. "Also, really cheap perfume. Yuck."

"Look at the grass," Ember said as they approached. "Someone moved the body, again."

"Right beside the tree," Cedric muttered. "You know what this means?"

"What?"

"That tree represents the county line. Whoever moved the body wanted to make sure that I would be the one to investigate."

Ember felt a chill run down her spine. If Cedric was right...

Her family could be in danger.

THIRTEEN

Cedric and Ember passed into the shade cast by the tall willow's gangly branches. Smothers looked up from the pad he scribbled upon and nodded.

"Morning, Sheriff, Ms. Ember. I've not moved from this spot since I called you."

"Good man." Cedric peered at the body on the ground. Like Olberman, she was face down. "Not the most practical attire for hiking out this way."

Ember noted the woman's revealing denim shorts and halter top. Her face remained obscured by grass, but Ember thought her blonde, pink-streaked hair seemed familiar.

"Do you know who this is, Smothers?" Cedric asked.

"Can't say I do," he said.

"It's Grace Fuller." Ember shook her head sadly. "We went to high school together, though we didn't really travel in the same circles."

"Fuller?" Cedric frowned. "The same Grace Fuller I picked up last year for prostitution?"

Ember nodded. "Sadly, yes. She used to pick up tricks at the Broom until I very nicely asked her to stop."

"I was always afraid she would end up like this," Kali said. "What a waste. She was always nice to me, fed me table scraps at the Broom."

"I know, Kali." Ember scooped up her familiar and hugged the cat to her body.

Cedric pursed his lips as he stared at the body. He crouched down and peeled the waistband of her shorts back enough to bare her lower back. Ember gasped at the sight of the familiar twin puncture wounds.

"That looks exactly like the ones we found on Olberman."

"I think you're right." Cedric stood up and put his hand on his hips. "This isn't good."

"Hey," Smothers said. "Here comes Agent Reddy."

Ember couldn't keep a scowl off her face as Cedric perked up. "Reddy's here? Good. He might have some insight."

"Oh, I'm sure he won't hesitate to share it," Ember grumbled.

Reddy approached and pumped hands with Cedric. "I got your call. You really think this has something to do with the Olberman killing?"

Cedric bent over and peeled the waistband away again. "See for yourself."

Reddy's face fell into a grave frown. "Oh, boy."

"Do you think we've got a serial killer on our hands?" Ember asked.

Reddy flinched. He turned stiffly to Cedric. "If you're going to bring the missus to crime scenes, can you at least coach her so she doesn't say things that might panic the public?"

"Excuse me, I'm standing right here," Ember said.

"Just pet your kitty, Miss Ember," Reddy said with a

wink. "Men are talking."

"They're going to call you Claude Balls instead of RU Reddy if you don't shut up, jerk," Kali hissed.

Cedric looked between Ember and Reddy, clearing torn. Instead of taking a stand for her, Cedric chose to change the subject.

"Look, R.U. These prong wounds look identical. No other obvious cause of death, the victim found face down in a deserted part of town. How can you not at least accept the possibility we're dealing with a sequence killing?"

"Oh, I can accept the possibility rightly enough, but it seems too tidy to me." Reddy gestured at the body. "I mean, if you were looking at a serial killer, they almost always pick one type of victim and stick to that exclusively. Olberman and this dead hussy don't have much in common other than both being white."

"This dead hussy has a name," Ember said coldly. "Grace Fuller. She was a local."

"And judging by that getup, she really got around." Reddy shook his head. "I don't buy it, Slick Rick. This is too convenient. Someone's trying to throw us off their trail by making it look like we've got a sequence killing."

Cedric's brow furrowed. "You really think they'd commit a second murder to cover up the first?"

"Oh yeah, for sure. I've seen it happen in cases I've worked before. Once you cross the line and take a human life, it gets easier every time. Besides, look at the tra—I mean, Miss Fuller here. Can you think of an easier target than a prostitute? Easy to lure them to an out-of-the-way place and do the deed."

Cedric didn't make any comment. He bent down low and sniffed deeply. Even in his human guise, Cedric's nose was incredibly keen. Whatever he scented on the corpse seemed to trouble him. His jaw set hard and he looked with worry toward Reddy.

Ember resolved to ask Cedric what he smelled later, when Reddy wasn't around. At least she knew Cedric's secret of being a Wolf shifter, and Reddy didn't. That counted for something.

"I'm telling you, Ric, this ain't a serial killer. This is someone who wanted Olberman dead and is covering their tracks."

"Just keep beating that dead horse, Reddy," Kali muttered.

Cedric walked a short distance away from Reddy while the agent crouched down and scrutinized Fuller's body. He arched his brows at Ember and she came to his side.

"What's wrong?"

"I recognize the scents on Fuller," he said. "Some of them, anyway."

Ember swallowed hard. "I see. Whose scents did you recognize?"

"Chad Whitman's, for one."

Ember gasped. "Then he's our killer!"

"Not necessarily, Ember." Cedric sighed. "He's not the only man I smell on her. There's about a dozen, some of which I don't recognize."

Ember's hopes fell. Fuller was a working girl, so to speak. It stood to reason she would have men's scents on her body. Whitman's scent was not proof of his guilt in and of itself. "Who else's scents do you recognize?"

"Well, I recognize one that bothers me a lot," Cedric replied, glancing over at Reddy.

"Who?"

"The same man whose property we're standing on right now. Hanky-Bob."

FOURTEEN

"Hanky-Bob?" Ember shook her head. "That doesn't make any sense."

"Hanky-Bob's a bachelor, Ember. Men, um, have needs."

"I know, you showed me evidence of that last night." Ember brushed her hip against him as she walked back over to Reddy. If his body remembered her, she'd be sure to give it plenty of chances.

Reddy straightened up, a purse held in his gloved hands. He opened the purse and took out a leather billfold.

"Whew," Reddy said, whistling as he counted the cash in the billfold. "Busy girl. There's over a grand in here."

"I think we can rule out robbery as a motivation," Cedric said.

"You think?" Reddy looked down at the body and the drag marks. "Looks like our vic was slain a dozen feet away and then dragged here. Why?"

"So I would be the one to investigate the crime," Cedric replied.

Reddy rolled his eyes. "Look at the ego on this guy.

C'mon, Slick Ric, you really think you're important enough to warrant this kind of attention?"

"Then why move the body to this exact spot?"

"Maybe he wanted to admire his handiwork in the shade? I don't know."

Cedric shook his head. "Lividity has set in. She's been dead for hours, at the very least. Most likely she was killed before dawn."

"Well, I'm not saying I have all the answers, Ric. I'm just saying I'm not ready to believe a cockamamie serial killer theory just yet."

"Yeah, because there's never been a serial killer in America before," Kali said. "How can Cedric stand this loser? Can't we cast a sneezing curse on him or something so he'll shut up for a while?"

"Hush, Kali," Ember said, scratching behind Kali's ear.

"Coroner's here," Cedric said.

"When will CSI arrive?" Reddy gestured at the wide, grassy field. "I want this area grid searched."

"We don't have CSI," Cedric said. "Smothers and I take care of it most of the time. When we need something done that we lack the equipment or knowledge to handle, we take it to the state trooper's lab."

"Fine." Reddy stood up and dusted off his hands. "I'll get some of my guys out here to do a grid search, then. It may not turn up anything, but maybe our boy was sloppy this time."

Reddy gazed about and scowled. "I feel like this area is familiar for some reason. Are we on someone's property, or is this unincorporated territory?"

"We're on Henry Robert's property, R.U." Ember thought Cedric spoke with exaggerated casualness.

"Hanky-Bob?" Reddy stiffened, his face growing red. "I should have figured that S.O.B. would be up to no good."

"Now, R.U.," Cedric said with patience. "You need to let bygones be bygones. That was a long time ago."

"How can you say that, when Hanky-Bob sold me that lemon of a Charger? I had to replace the entire engine before it was all said and done, and it still leaked oil."

"He told you to let him put a new engine in it."

"He also told me the engine it had could go for another fifty thousand miles, too." Reddy shook his head. "But you're right, Ric. I can't let my own prejudice interfere with the investigation. I promise I'll give him a fair shake, all right?"

Cedric didn't look convinced. Ember knew she, herself, was not. Cedric sighed. "Fair enough. Let's go talk to him."

They drove the short distance to Hanky-Bob's property. Unlike Chad Whitman, Hanky-Bob didn't fence off his property. You just trundled along an undulating gravel road and suddenly came upon his compound in the woods. Hanky-Bob had more garages than he had houses. More than two-dozen vehicles in various states of repair lurked beneath American flag tarps.

Hanky-Bob came out of his garage wearing grease-stained overalls and no shirt to hide the wiry hairs on his chest and arms. He smiled at Cedric and Ember as Agent Reddy parked.

"Hey, Cedric, Ember. What brings you out this way? Need another hotrod?"

Cedric's smile was strained. "Hello, Hanky-Bob. I wish I were here on so cheerful an errand as that."

Agent Reddy strode up to join them. Hanky-Bob's smile faded. "Who's this?"

"Surely you recognize me, Hank," Reddy said, taking off his sunglasses. "Even though I've had a haircut."

"Holy crap, R.U. Reddy?" Hanky-Bob grinned. "How've you been?"

Reddy didn't answer for a long moment. "Are you aware there's a body on your property?"

"A body?" Hanky-Bob's mouth dropped open. "No, of course I didn't know. I'd have called Cedric here if I'd known."

"Is that a fact?" Reddy's eyes narrowed. "What were you up to last night, Hank? Not to mention two nights ago."

"Wait..." Hanky-Bob glanced over at Cedric. "Hey, am I a suspect? I didn't know nothin' about the body on my property, all right?"

Cedric sighed. "Just answer his question, Hanky-Bob. It'll go a lot easier if you do."

Hanky-Bob shifted uncomfortably. "I was here, working on the Mustang. Both nights."

"Was anyone here with you who can confirm that?" Reddy asked.

Hanky-Bob shook his head. "No, I was alone."

Ember and Cedric exchanged glances. Hanky-Bob usually had at least half a dozen guests at any given time, friends who would drink beer and take apart cars with him. Being alone that time of night wasn't just unusual for him, it was out of character.

"You know a woman by the name of Grace Fuller, Hank?" Reddy asked.

Hanky-Bob's cheeks flushed. "Gracie? I—I might have run into her a couple times in town. Why?"

Reddy grinned. "Don't worry about it. Mind if I take a look around?"

Hanky-Bob frowned. "Don't you need a warrant?" He turned to Cedric. "Doesn't he have to have a warrant?"

"Well, not necessarily, Hanky-Bob," Cedric replied carefully. "I mean, if you give him permission he can look without a warrant. Otherwise, he has to have one."

Hanky-Bob set his jaw hard. "Then I don't give him permission."

Reddy's face twitched a sneer. "I'll be in touch, Hank. Don't leave town."

"I don't even live in town," Hanky-Bob snapped back.

As they strode back to their respective cars, Reddy glared at Cedric. "Nice going, Slick Ric. Whose side are you on, anyway?"

Ember and Cedric watched as Reddy tore out of the gravel lot. She had a feeling Reddy was only just beginning to be a thorn in their sides.

FIFTEEN

Ember and Cedric drove away from the tense meeting in silence. Cedric's eyes seemed distant as he stared at the road ahead.

"Hanky-Bob was hiding something, wasn't he?" Ember asked.

Cedric nodded. "I got that impression as well."

"What do you think he was hiding?" Kali asked. "Hanky-Bob's a hick, but he's always struck me as harmless."

Cedric shook his head. "I don't know. I'm hoping it was just because he, um, spent some time with Grace Fuller in a... professional sense."

Ember felt a bit of relief. Maybe it was just that. "Let's hope so. I'd hate to think of him getting into some kind of trouble."

"Me, too. I don't see Hanky-Bob as a killer, though. I just don't. It doesn't fit his personality at all."

"I know what you mean, but..." Ember swallowed hard. "He did seem to really hate Olberman. Almost started a fight in my Pub over it, in fact."

Cedric glanced sharply at me. "That's not going to look good if Reddy finds out."

"Of course Reddy is going to find out. That guy's relentless, and he has a grudge against Hanky-Bob. It's obvious. Shouldn't he recuse himself or something?"

"Can't rightly say how the FBI does things, but Reddy won't put Hanky-Bob away for this. Not unless he's convinced it really was Hanky-Bob who killed Olberman and Grace."

"I hope you're right. For Bob's sake." Ember felt for certain there was more to the killings than Reddy wanted to believe, but had no idea how to go about proving her point to the obstinate man.

They drove back into town and pulled up in front of the police station. The press no longer mobbed the parking lot, though they still maintained a presence. Several news vans sat outside on the street, and she spotted Kelly milling around by the drug store.

Ember and Cedric entered the station and prepared to await the arrival of the coroner. Doctor Dalton had patients that morning but promised to be along before lunch.

"Where's Smothers?" Ember asked, looking about the tiny station. "His car was out front."

Cedric chuckled. "Where do you think?"

Ember sighed. "You know he just goes in there to get on Facebook and Twitter, right?"

"At least, we HOPE it's social media and not something...unsavory," Kali said.

Cedric shrugged. "If I have to use the restroom, I'll kick him out. It's not really a problem, yet. Besides, I need someone doing that social media thing in the department as I have no intention."

Ember was about to ask why when the bathroom door

slammed open. Smothers waddled out into the lobby, toilet paper stuck to his shoe and his fly undone.

"Sheriff! You've got to see this." He shuffled up to Cedric and Ember, showing them his phone screen.

"What am I looking at, here?" Cedric asked.

"The City Hall's Facebook page. I moderate it, remember? Well, check out what someone posted on our wall."

Smothers pressed his pudgy finger on the play key, and the video began. An obviously computer generated gridwork background made Ember frown.

"Is this a video game?" she asked.

"If it is, it has some seriously dated graphics," Kali quipped. "I've seen PS2 games with better rendering."

"Just keep watching." Smothers turned the volume up. As the volume bar flashed off the screen, a rendered image of a person doing cartwheels appeared. It flipped into the center of the gridwork room and stopped, a garish smile stretched over its thin face.

"Is that like a Jester's costume?" Cedric asked.

"I think so, but why?"

"Here it comes," Smothers said eagerly. The Jester produced a sign, like Wile E. Coyote. The message scrawled on its digital surface proved simple.

Foolkiller 2, Cops 0

"Oh boy," Cedric said, letting out a long, exasperated sigh. "Oh boy, oh boy, oh boy."

"You can go ahead and curse, dear," Ember said. "Get it out of your system."

Cedric followed her advice, growing so creative in his swearing Smothers blushed.

"Looks like we might have a serial killer after all," Ember replied.

"Good luck convincing Reddy," Cedric sighed. "He'll

just say it's a smokescreen again, or unrelated. Which, honestly, it might be. There's no guarantee that whoever made and uploaded this video is the killer, or even knows who is."

Smothers nodded. "Like when there's an explosion, and, even when it's not a bomb, six terrorist organizations call to claim it was them?"

"Could be a plea for attention, right." Cedric blew air out through his nostrils and growled as he watched the video again.

"That's what your head says," Ember cocked an eyebrow at Cedric. "What does your gut say?"

Cedric looked at her grimly. "My gut says this isn't a hoax or a plea for attention, or even a smokescreen."

Ember nodded. "Mine, too."

"Mine three," Kali said.

She turned to Smothers. "You're our resident computer expert, Deputy Smothers. Is there any way we can track down the person who uploaded this video?"

Smothers frowned as he took his phone back. "I can try, but, the fact of the matter is, there's a lot of ways to cover your tracks online. If he used an Onion router, or hid his IP address, it could be next to impossible.

Cedric rubbed his chin thoughtfully. "I'm going to call Reddy. Get his tech guys on this ASAP. No offense, Smothers, but we've got to catch this guy if we can."

Ember thought of the CGI jester and shuddered. It very well may have been the avatar of a real life killer.

Ember couldn't shake the feeling that things were going to get worse before they got better.

SIXTEEN

Ember caught a ride with Smothers back to the house to pick up her car, then drove to the Broken Broom. She found Ash and Willow cleaning up after the breakfast rush. Ember waited and watched, checking on Willow's progress. To her eyes, it didn't seem Willow was especially slow as she swept up the lobby.

She entered through the rear kitchen doors. Ash glanced up from the dishwasher.

"You finally made it. Who died?"

"Grace Fuller. Did you know her?"

Ash's face fell. "Oh no. Yes, I did know her, though not very well. I heard, um, she was, shall we say, alternatively employed—"

"She was a prostitute, if that's what you're tap dancing around."

Ash sighed. "I don't want to judge, I really don't. Was it one of her, um, clients who did her in?"

Ember went to help her unload the dishwasher. "Unclear, as of yet. She has the same wounds on her back as

Olberman, and, so far, it looks like the cause of death may have been the same as well."

"Does that mean we have a serial killer?"

Ember pointed at Ash, glad to be validated. "That's exactly what I said! R.U. Reddy keeps saying it's a smokescreen."

"What a jerk."

Ember sighed. "I'd like to agree, but, the fact is, he's just trying to do his job. Besides, he might be right. Olberman had plenty of enemies, and...I hate to say it, but there are some people who think Grace's life wasn't worth much because of her profession."

"True, but it could be a serial killer."

"Reddy said they tend to go for one type of victim. You know, like that strangler guy always picked women who looked like his ex-wife?"

"They don't all pick exactly the same kinds of victims, I don't think. I don't know. I'm not the detective in the family. Still, looks like a serial killer to me."

They shared a chuckle before Ember went out to check on Willow. The floor looked pretty good, though she'd missed a salt packet under one of the tables.

"Looking good, Willow. Grab the salt packet from under table four and give us a mop, will you?"

"Sure thing, Miss Ember." Willow went and retrieved the packet, starting to throw it in the ceramic bin holding the others.

"Gross," Kali said.

"Wait, Willow. Just throw it away. It's been on the floor."

"Oh, okay."

Ember watched as Willow moved off to retrieve the

mop and bucket. At least she had a good attitude, even if she wasn't quick on the uptake.

Ember helped with the lunch rush and clean up. She lingered with Ash and looked over the grimoire for a while, though their efforts bore little fruit. Ember reiterated her stance that they needed to create a new spell to restore Cedric's memories.

"It's so dangerous, Ember! What if we summon a demon from the ninth level of Hell, or tear a hole in the fabric of reality?"

"Then we'll kick the demon's butt and patch the hole," Kali said. "We're not powerless, you know."

"We'll be careful," Ember said. "By keeping our base enchantment simple, there's little chance of it getting out of hand."

"We've both heard stories..."

"I know, but most of those custom spells that went wrong were designed to do something outrageous anyway. Like making gold out of thin air or giving absolute dominion over humanity. Of course, the magic went wrong. If you're going to manipulate reality, you keep it small scale."

Ash checked her phone. "If you say so. Shouldn't you get going to pick up April from afterschool?"

Ember frowned. "Yes, I probably should. I have to drop off the check. Love you, Sis."

"Love you, too. Be careful, in case there really is a serial killer."

"I will."

Ember drove to the elementary school, pulling around back because she knew, in nice weather, the children would be on the playground. She parked in the gravel lot and walked over to the chain link fence around the playground area.

"Hello," said the program's director, a middle-aged woman who was also the school's secretary.

"Hello, Margaret." Ember pulled out her checkbook. "Um, I have the payment, but I don't have a pen..."

"Say no more. I'll go grab you one off the clipboard." Margaret strode across the playground while Ember waited at the fence. April hadn't noticed her yet, being busy on the slide structure.

A pair of girls sat in the sandbox not far from where Ember stood. They were repeating nursery rhymes in unison. Ember chuckled, remembering when the Kindergarten teacher had made her learn those same rhymes.

"Monday's Child is fair of Face," said the girls. "Tuesdays' Child is Full of Grace. Wednesday's child is..."

Ember's eyes went wide. The checkbook fell from her nerveless fingers. Tuesday's child is full of grace...Fuller, Grace.

Grace Fuller. No, it had to be her overactive mind, grasping for straws. Besides, Olberman didn't sound remotely like 'fair of face.'

She couldn't get her mind off the notion, however, churning it over during the drive home. While she and Cedric prepared dinner in the kitchen, and April played in the living room, she brought up her notion, albeit sheepishly.

Cedric set a case of pork chops on the counter and frowned thoughtfully. "I think Reddy's shaken your confidence, Ember. That's actually a really good idea."

"I don't know. It doesn't fit Olberman."

"True." Cedric turned back to season the chops and she grated carrots for a salad. They worked in silence for a time, until Cedric gasped and turned around excitedly to face her.

"Wait a minute...what's the Monday Rhyme again?"

"Monday's child is fair of face, why?"

"Just a second..." Cedric dug out his phone and tapped on the screen. After a moment he turned it to face her. Olberman stood on the cover of his autobiography, entitled *Mr. Monday Morning*. "That's been his nickname ever since."

"Reddy will never buy it."

"He might, because I'm not done." Cedric showed her photos of Olberman's body at the softball field. "Look, we know Olberman died over here, in foul ball territory. Then they dragged his body until just his head was in fair territory. He's literally 'fair of face.'"

Emer sucked in air through her teeth. "Oh, boy. This could get really, really bad."

SEVENTEEN

Ember moved about the lobby floor at the Broom, balancing a coffee cup in one hand and a tray of her famous loaded hash browns in the other. She stopped to refill depleted coffee mugs along her way to table seven, where she deposited the hash browns.

All about her, a quiet buzz of conversation hovered at or around the murders. Olberman's death had been sensational enough, but, now that a local girl had joined the body count, everyone had a theory.

"We all know it was them dirty Reds," said Spuds McCormick, an aging war veteran whose bluster far exceeded his willingness to back it up with facts, let alone fists. "I mean, read the clues. Them commies can't stand the idea of a successful businessman."

"You're talking out your rear again, Spuds," snapped his eternally bickering companion, Ned Jackson. "Ridiculous conspiracy theories about the Chinese, please. We all know it was aliens."

Ember filled his cup and couldn't help but join the conversation. "What makes you say it was aliens, Ned?"

"Well, you know how I go out to Miller's Point and do my frog hunting? Well, the other night I looked up in the air and this flying saucer was just hovering there. I'm lucky I didn't get abducted and anally probed."

Spuds sneered. "Is this the same night you saw the house on giant chicken legs, or were you on a different moonshine trip that time?"

"I saw what I saw, Spuds…"

Ember left them to it and returned to the kitchen, where Ash attempted to show Willow how to make the pub's famous buttermilk biscuits.

"Don't squish the butter between your fingers, you'll heat it up that way. Use the claw hand." Ash picked up flour-shrouded chunks of butter and let them drop back into the bowl. "See?"

"I think so, Miss Ash."

"Good. Keep going until you've got crumbs about the size of peas. Then I'll show you what comes next."

Ember motioned Ash over. Kali lounged in her customary spot on the unused prep table in the corner, snoring softly as they spoke.

"So, how's our new recruit doing?"

"Better?" Ash sighed. "She's not the sharpest rock in the box, but she's got some of it down. I just have to show her everything. And I do mean everything."

"I know, but remember what we were like in our first jobs? Learning how to work is a thing."

"Yeah, if the schools spent more time on teaching kids how to work, instead of the pythagorean theorem and Chaucer, the world would be a better place. Thanks for coming in this morning."

"No problem. Doc Dalton can't perform the exam on

our latest vic until this afternoon, so there's not much call for me at the moment."

"You know, even if Willow works out, we're still going to need some more hands here. Maybe Sage could--?"

"I hate to take her away from her general store, and she's been spending every spare moment with her boyfriend, Big Tobacco. I barely see her anymore."

Ash cocked an eyebrow. "You two haven't quite been the same since the Glawkus caper."

"I know. I feel bad, but the Glawkus looked so much like Sage in her hybrid form. I guess I should have trusted her all along."

"Have you told Sage this yet?"

Ember shook her head. "No."

"Then you probably should."

Ember picked Kali up, cradling the sleepy cat to her chest. "I'm going to pop in at the station, and bring Cedric his lunch. Will you be alright until I get back?"

"Yeah, me and the kid can handle it." Ash winked. "Go be Sherlock Holmes. Save the day."

"Yeah, right," Ember chuckled. She deposited Kali in the back seat, where the cat promptly snuggled up with a towel she'd used to cover her steering wheel in the hot Louisiana sun.

She drove to the station, trying to connect the victims in her head. A rich industrialist, and a small-town working girl. Other than gaining the general scorn of society, neither seemed the least bit alike.

Ember remembered one of the main mantras of murder investigation, namely that people rarely killed people they didn't know. Who in the world would be in the same circle of friends as Olberman and Fuller? It didn't make sense.

The only thing that did make sense was her theory was

right, and the killings were the work of a sequence murderer. Ember didn't want it to be true, not really, but she had a gut feeling it was.

Ember carried the lunch into the station house, Kali draped over her shoulder. She found Cedric in his office talking to R.U. Reddy.

"I brought your lunch, dear," Ember said, smiling at Cedric and ignoring Reddy.

"Thanks," Cedric took the bag from her and smiled back. "I was just discussing your theory with Agent Reddy."

"Oh?" Ember turned her gaze toward Reddy. "Is that so?"

"It unfortunately is," Reddy said, a trace of scorn creeping into his tone. "Look, I know you've seen lots of detective shows on television, but real serial killers are very rare."

"What about the rhyme, and the victims? It makes sense." Ember struggled to keep her tone civil, but hostility crept into her words. "How do you explain the fact Olberman was dragged until just his face was in fair territory, then?"

"We don't know what went through the killer's mind in that field. All we have is supposition."

"Tuesday's Child is Full of Grace. Grace Fuller? You don't think that at least bears some looking into?"

"Nope, not one bit."

"Would you stop discounting every word that comes out of my mouth?" Ember's voice rang in the air of the tidy office. Cedric swallowed, looking anxious. Ember cringed inwardly. She hadn't intended to be so loud.

"You know what?" Agent Reddy glared at her as he spoke. "Sheriff Jamison can run his station any way he wants, I guess, but, in the FBI, we don't make a habit of involving civilians in our investigations. Wifey can go home now."

Ember's eyes bulged in their sockets. She looked to Cedric, hoping he would say something. He appeared at a loss, tracking his gaze between Ember and Reddy.

Ember turned and stormed out of the office, greatly disturbing Kali.

"Thanks for sticking up for me, Cedric," she snapped right before slamming the door.

EIGHTEEN

"What happened?" Kali asked groggily. "Are you mad at Cedric for some reason?"

"Why would I be mad at him? Just because he sat there like a bump on a log while his buddy R.U. Reddy talked down to me and kicked me off the case? Out of the station even? Of course I'm not mad."

"Ouch." Kali leaped off her shoulder into the open window of the car and settled into the front seat. "Yeah, that's kind of a bummer."

"I wish I could see to it Reddy wakes up tomorrow on a scratchy lily pad." Ember peeled out in the parking lot, startling Kali.

"Settle down, Speed Racer! Don't drive angry, so they say."

Ember sighed, forcing herself to be calm. "Sorry, Kali."

She drove to the Broom, and found the lunch rush to be tepid at best. Ash and Willow seemed to be getting along well, since laughter emanated from the kitchen.

Ash's smile faded when she saw Ember's face. "Oh no. What happened?"

Ember explained, and Ash grew outraged on her behalf. "Stupid FBI. Come in like gangbusters and fart all over everything in their path."

"So, I guess the good news is I'll be able to help with the lunch and dinner rushes."

"There is no lunch rush...in fact, we don't really need you here." Ash's eyes glittered with intent. "Why don't you go and stop by the General Store, say hello to Sage? You guys could get a coffee or something, reconnect. You could vent. It would be cathartic."

Ember wanted to argue but changed her mind. "Kali, are you coming along?"

"No, I'm good," Kali said as Willow stroked her behind the ears. "Oh yeah, that's the spot."

"I'll be back in a bit," Ember said, taking her purse and heading back to the parking lot. She made the short drive to Sage's store, feeling apprehension twist her gut the entire way. Sage had been a good friend of Ember's for many years, but the Glawkus caper had driven a wedge between them.

Ember pushed the doors open, the smell of feed and cedar chips reaching her nostrils. She smiled when she saw the gaggle of freshly hatched chicks waddling around in a chicken wire enclosure. She stepped closer, eyes wide and adoring. A heat lamp buzzed as it beamed warmth down on the chicks.

"Go ahead, pick one up. You know you want to."

Ember glanced over and saw Sage's smiling face. They moved together and hugged. Ember held on a bit longer than normal, and Sage cocked an eyebrow when they finally parted.

"What's up?"

Ember sighed. "Listen, back when Cedric lost his

memory, and I was going a little bit crazy, I said some things I shouldn't have. I never should have doubted you, Sage. I never should have accused you. You're my best friend."

Sage smiled, her eyes shining. "Thank you. It's all right, I know you were going through a lot."

"I just didn't want there to be bad blood between us," Ember went on.

"Oh, there could never be bad blood here, not really. We've been through too much. I guess I might have given that impression, with how much I've been hanging out with Tobacco."

Ember cocked an eyebrow. "How are you guys doing?"

Sage smiled. "Good…I'm not sure where it's going, or how long it's going to last, but I'm happy."

Ember returned the smile. "If you're happy, I'm happy. I mean, Tobacco is…you know."

"A little person?" Ash chuckled. "Believe me, that's never been a problem. Not all of his body parts are stumpy. He looks like a pole vaulter when—"

"Enough! Stop! Shut up!" Ember clamped her hands over her ears. "That's not what I meant at all! I was trying to say that he's a bit of a rambling man, that's all."

"Oh. Well, I guess we know where my mind is." Sage chuckled.

"Hey, you want to grab a cup of coffee?"

Sage glanced around. "Sure, I can lock up for a bit."

"I thought you hired someone to help out?"

"I did, they just ghosted me and stopped showing up for work."

Ember's eyes narrowed and Sage laughed.

"They're not dead, they picked up their last check on Friday. Not everything is a mystery needing to be solved, Poirot."

Ember laughed softly. It felt good to be back with Sage again. They spent a few minutes oohing and aahing over the cute, fuzzy chicks, then headed across the street to Kathy's Korner Café.

Kathy came out of the office and sat with them while they sipped coffee and nibbled on watercress sandwiches. They all agreed that Agent R.U. Reddy was a jerk for throwing Ember out.

"You know what would shut that Reddy guy up right quick?" Sage asked. "If we figured out who the next victim might be and stopped the murder in its tracks."

Ember laughed. "I don't think anything is going to change his opinion of me, but I agree we should be thinking about who the next victim might be."

"What's the next line of the poem?"

"Wednesday's Child is Full of Woe."

"Well, that sounds easy." Sage spread her hands out wide. "We just have to figure out who in town has been through a lot of crap in their life."

Ember grunted, tapping the table with her fingers. Someone who'd suffered a lot...try as she might, the only person she could come up with was April.

"April's been through so much," Ember said. "But you don't think the killer would go after a first grader, do you?"

All three women exchanged glances. Ember stood up suddenly, her heart pounding in her chest.

"I need to pick up April. Now."

She scooped up Kali and headed out the door.

NINETEEN

Ember forced herself not to run back to her car. All round her, the sights and cheery sounds of downtown Caucherie seemed to mock her urgency with their laconic small-town aplomb.

"You're holding me really tight," Kali said.

"Sorry." Ember relaxed her grip. "Better?"

"Yes. Don't worry, I'm sure April is fine. Most serial killers don't go after children..." Kali swallowed. "Except the Atlanta killer, and BTK, and...I'm just going to shut up now. Sorry."

"You're fine, Kali. Ignoring the truth doesn't make it go away."

"If it did, we cats would basically be Gods," Kali said. "Or should I say, bigger Gods than we already are."

Ember knew Kali was trying to cheer her up, but apprehension still roiled in her gut.

It was ridiculous to think the killer would go after April...or was it? Her struggles were a matter of public record. Whoever the killer was—and Ember was convinced she was right, and the murders were the work of a sequence murderer—they obviously knew a lot about the town and its people.

It wasn't outside the realm of reason that April might find herself a target on the Jester's list.

Ember struggled to keep her speed under control as she headed for the elementary school. It was hard, with even the cheerful sun seemingly diminished by the terror gnawing at her belly. April had been through so much. She didn't deserve any of it, and now...

"Um, you're up over forty and this road has a lot of turns... " Kali said.

"Darn it. Sorry, I'm just--"

"Worried, I know."

Ember decided to speed. If Smothers pulled her over—which he probably wouldn't, he knew her car—she would explain the situation.

"Now you're up over fifty."

"I know. I'll be careful, I promise."

Ember called the school on her way but got no answer. That wasn't unusual, in and of itself, because Margaret had to range around the playground and the cordless phone's signal only reached past the monkey bars.

Still, it added fuel to the growing fire of paranoia in her belly. Ember skidded into the parking lot and rolled to a lurching stop near the cyclonic fence gate.

Margaret spotted her and came to the gate, a smile on her face. "Hello, Ember. Didn't you get April already?"

"No," Ember said firmly. "I haven't."

Margaret's brow furrowed with confusion. "I haven't seen her around in a bit, but I'm sure she's out here somewhere. Let me go find her."

Margaret searched the playground for April, calling the girl's name. Ember fought a new wave of panic. She kept hoping to see April's head pop out of a hooded slide, or from behind one of the trees providing shade for the playground.

When Margaret came back to the gate, it was at a jog. She grabbed her sign out clipboard and pored over it.

"She hasn't been signed out," Margaret said with alarm. "I—I don't know where she is. Maybe she got inside the building somehow?"

Ember's belly twisted in knots. "Can you call me if you find her? I'm going to go home and see if, maybe, Cedric picked her up."

Ember knew it was a vain hope at best. Cedric almost never picked April up from the afterschool program because his day ended late. As Margaret rushed off, Ember considered her options.

She decided to try a locator spell. Ember clambered around in her back seat, trying to find something that belonged to April so she could focus her magic. To her relief, her fingers closed on a pink hair tie with plastic butterflies.

Ember channeled the magical energy through her body as she chanted under her breath, holding the hair tie tightly. Locator magics were tricky, and difficult to focus. The temptation to use Dark Magic to ease her search throbbed strongly in Ember's mind. It would be so easy...

She forced the thought from her head, and concentrated on her spell. It spread out in an invisible nimbus around her. The eldritch umbrella spread out to encompass the school and surrounding area and fizzled out.

"Come on," Ember slammed her fist into the steering wheel. She grabbed her phone and dialed Cedric. When he didn't answer she angrily tossed her phone down on the center console and started the car. Kali ducked under the errantly aimed missile and yelped.

"Watch it!"

"Sorry. It was supposed to land on the seat."

"I already caught an urn with my spine this week, jeez."

"I'm so sorry." Ember reached out to scratch her familiar on the head, though it brought her little comfort.

Ember's heart raced the whole way home. She kept thinking of how awful it would be to get the notice of another body, and to find April laying face down on the ground. Who could possibly be enough of a monster to electrocute a first grader, especially if it took three long minutes?

"Please let her be alright," Ember prayed to the Celestial Powers that Be. "Please. Mess with me all you want, but don't make that little girl suffer more than she already has. Please."

The one thing that kept Ember from degenerating into a panic was Munkilok. If April got into trouble, at least the Imp could take over her body and possibly find a way to escape.

It seemed to take inordinately long to reach home. Every person on the highway ahead of her went about ten miles under the limit. When she tried to pass, they sped up until she was forced to return to the lane because of oncoming traffic.

Ember turned into their driveway at last, skidding to a halt and leaping out of her car. The cooling engine made pops and hisses as she rushed to the porch and flung open the front door.

"Cedric? Cedric!" She ran inside. "April is...."

Ember's voice trailed off as she beheld April sitting in front of the TV, eating cheese puffs.

"Hi, Miss Ember," she said.

"April." Ember ran over and hugged the girl, unmindful

of the streaks of orange the girl's hands and face left on her. "Thank goodness you're all right."

"Why wouldn't I be all right?"

Cedric came in from the back porch, dusting his hands off. "Hey, I finally changed that light bulb—"

Ember grabbed him by the shirt and shook him. "Did you pick up April from afterschool?"

"Yeah, I did. Reddy had an appointment to keep, and I thought I'd save you the trouble."

Ember let out a strangled growl. "And you didn't think about calling me and telling me you had her? Not only that, but you didn't sign her out! Poor Margaret is losing her mind."

Cedric winced. "I'll call her."

Ember waited while Cedric called the school and profusely apologized for not signing April out. When he finished, he faced Ember with a somber frown. "I'm sorry. I should have told you I got her, not to mention signed her out."

"Thank you." Ember sighed. "I'm just glad she's safe."

Ember noticed the chicken thawing on the counter. "I thought we were having leftover spaghetti tonight?"

"I thought I'd roast a chicken, instead. Maybe do some mashed potatoes, since Reddy is coming for dinner."

"What?" Ember blurted.

"Reddy's coming over for dinner. That's not a problem, is it?"

"Oh snap," Kali said. "It's about to go down!"

TWENTY

Ember's eyes narrowed to slits. "You're darn right it's a problem! I don't want that man in my house."

"Ember, please—"

She jabbed a finger in his face. "Don't you 'Ember, please' me, Cedric. You think I've forgotten how you just sat there and let him talk to me like that, then kick me out of your office? It was insulting, degrading, and, worst of all, you let me down. Do you have any idea how I feel right now?"

Cedric's lips became a thin, tight line. "I do. I do know how you feel. I'm sorry I didn't stick up for you, Ember. I know I should have, but...but..."

"But R.U. Reddy is your buddy, and bros before hos, am I right?"

Cedric sighed. "Do you have to say that word in front of April?"

"What word, Ho?" April asked with a sinister laugh. "I've heard worse than that, Wolf Boy."

They turned to find Munkilok sitting backwards on the living room's stuffed sofa. April's orange-streaked face appeared all the more twisted for the sly, knowing grin on her face.

"Oh no, not this guy, again," Kali sighed. "Why don't you go possess something that matches your personality? Like a possum's behind?"

Ember ignored Kali's acerbic tongue and addressed the imp.

"Munkilok, why are you here? April's not in danger."

Munkilok let out a laugh. "Not physical danger, but didn't you know it scares her when you two fight?"

Ember felt a stab of pathos, as if she failed the little girl. Cedric glared at the imp wearing April's body.

"We don't fight all that much," Cedric said.

"Oh, is that what you think?" Munkilok laughed. "It's like watching a reality TV show around these parts. I'm like, 'what will these two idiots do next?' If I could film this crap, I'd be a millionaire."

Cedric looked abashed. Munkilok laughed a final time and turned around to devour cheese puffs with noisy gusto. Cedric turned to Ember, his eyes full of worry.

"Do we fight a lot?"

"Probably more...ever since you lost your memory." Ember sighed. She looked up at Cedric and glared, though she kept her tone civil enough. "I still can't believe you invited him to dinner, after what he said."

"He was out of line, no doubt," Cedric said. "I intend to handle it."

"Oh, you're going to handle it," Ember said with a growl. "I feel so much better now. What, you're going to cook him dinner, pour him wine, and then beg him to be nicer to your wife? That's really taking a stand, Cedric."

Cedric closed his jaw. "I wish you could just trust me."

Ember rolled her eyes. "Oh, fine. You go ahead, put your plan into motion."

Cedric sighed. "Would you mind peeling the potatoes for me?"

"Yes, I would mind. I'll endure this man in my home, even though he insulted me, because I know it's important to you. But I'm not lifting a finger to feed him. You're on your own, buddy."

Ember left Cedric before he could respond. She took April—back in control of her body again—to wash up her hands and face before they settled in for homework.

"Miss Ember," April said while they studied her history assignment. "Why did the colonists dress up like native Americans to throw the tea into the harbor?"

"I guess they were in disguise," Ember said, half distracted by her anger with Cedric and Reddy.

"Didn't they know that was cultural 'propriation?" April asked.

Ember laughed, and stroked April's golden hair. "Appropriation. And no, I don't think that occurred to them. People didn't used to be as nice as they are now."

"You mean like when they owned slaves?"

Ember nodded. "Right. Not everybody was mean, though. In fact, did you know our state actually split in two because so many nice people didn't want to own slaves?"

The doorbell rang and Ember sighed. "I guess our dinner guest is here. We'll finish this up after we eat, okay?"

"Okay."

Ember headed down to the kitchen as Reddy entered her home. He smiled and shook hands with Cedric before turning his gaze her way.

"Miss Ember. I hope I didn't upset you too much this

afternoon. I'm just trying to maintain professional decorum."

Ember didn't answer. She just helped April seat herself at the table as Cedric worked on serving dinner. He and Reddy kept up a constant stream of chatter, most of it completely unrelated to the case.

"Here's the thing, Slick Ric," Reddy said around a mouthful of garlic-roasted chicken. "I'm not saying everyone in Red Bud is sleeping with their cousins...I'm just saying the gene pool could use a little chlorine."

They laughed together, but Ember noted Cedric had a hard edge to his eyes. Cedric kept glancing at the clock on the wall as well, and then toward the front door. What was he up to? Ember thought perhaps he'd ordered a fancy dessert and expected delivery soon.

Reddy's laughter died down, and he turned toward Ember. "Ember, I really hope there's not bad blood between us. I just don't believe a civilian should be involved in an ongoing investigation, unless they're a suspect or a witness of course."

Cedric set his wine glass down with an audible thump. "You're right, R.U."

Ember scowled. She was supposed to trust Cedric, and he sat there agreeing with Reddy?

The doorbell rang, and Cedric got to his feet, dabbing his mouth with a napkin briefly. "I'll get that."

"Who's here?" Ember asked.

Cedric opened the door, and an elderly brown-skinned man in a pale green suit entered the living room.

"Mayor Stubbs?" Ember gasped.

What's he doing here?

TWENTY-ONE

Mayor Stubbs smiled warmly at Ember as he moved into the kitchen. She frowned at the dry-cleaning bag in his hand, wondering if he were in the middle of errands.

"Good evening, all," he said. "Sorry to disturb y'all's dinner--oh, hello, Kitty." Stubbs reached down to give Kali a few stroking pats. Kali purred warmly. She'd always liked Mayor Stubbs, probably because he fed her catfish nuggets as a kitten.

"It's no trouble." Reddy stood up and swiftly crossed the room to shake the Mayor's hand. "Agent Robert Ulysses Reddy, Federal Bureau of Investigation."

"I remember you, Reddy," Stubbs cackled. "You shoved a cherry bomb down the toilets in the men's room back when I was the assistant principal at the high school."

Reddy laughed. "I'd forgotten all about that. Mr. Stubbs...I guess it's Mayor Stubbs, now."

"Not for much longer." Stubbs disengaged from Reddy and turned toward Ember.

"What brings you out this way, Mayor?" Ember asked,

still eyeing the dry-cleaning bag. "Can I take your bag for the time being?"

"Certainly." Stubbs handed it over to her. Ember felt its weight and couldn't fathom what type of garment might be in the bag. "As far as why I'm here, well, maybe I should let Cedric explain that part of it."

Ember and Reddy turned to face Cedric. Cedric's eyes grew fierce, lighting up with a challenge as he stared intently at Reddy.

"Since you objected so strongly to having a civilian involved in the case, you'll be happy to know I've taken steps to rectify the situation."

Reddy frowned, holding his hand up, palm facing out. "Now see here, Ric. I'm not trying to get your wife in trouble with the mayor. I'm fine with her recusing herself this afternoon."

Ember turned to Stubbs and cocked an eye. "Am I in trouble?"

Stubbs laughed warmly. "Oh, yes. You're in all kinds of trouble, just not the kind you think."

Ember liked Mayor Stubbs—everyone did, almost universally—but she grew tired of the cryptic exchanges flashing around her kitchen.

"Okay, would someone like to explain exactly what's going on here before I lose my mind?" Ember glanced among the three men, her eyes narrowed with suspicion.

Cedric cleared his throat. "Well, I asked Mayor Stubbs to stop by tonight for a very specific reason."

He raced over to the bookshelf, aware Ember's patience wore thin, and took down a copy of the Bible. Ember was surprised by that, since neither of them was terribly religious. He presented the bible to the Mayor, who held it out flat in front of him on his palms.

"Ember, would you please put your hands on the Good Book, please?"

Ember frowned, glancing at Cedric. Cedric nodded his head.

"Ember McNair-Jamison, do you accept the duties and responsibilities of a Deputy of our fine county in the great state of Louisiana?"

Ember's jaw dropped open. "What?"

"You're being deputized," Cedric said. "I still have the right to swear people in temporarily, but..."

Cedric cast a withering glare at Reddy. "Circumstances dictated that I have the Mayor make it long term."

Ember's eyes narrowed. "Yes," she said fiercely. "Yes, I accept."

"Excellent." Mayor Stubbs tucked the bible under his arm and smiled. "Well, my job here is done. I have to get back to the missus."

Ember looked at the bag draped over the back of their sofa. "Wait, what about your bag?"

"That's not my bag. It's yours."

Ember frowned in confusion. She opened the bag and laughed when she saw a brown uniform inside.

"If it doesn't fit, my missus will do alterations for free," Stubbs said with a wink.

Ember followed Stubbs outside, silently gloating even though she didn't want to make a display of it.

"Thank you so much, Mr. Mayor."

"Think nothing of it. I can honestly say it's one of my favorite duties I've performed thus far."

Ember's jaw worked silently as she struggled with herself. "Um, if you don't mind my asking, why are you quitting the Mayor gig? You're not...you're not sick, are you?"

Stubbs laughed. "Naw, I'm fine. Hale and hearty with the body of a man twenty years my junior. No, the missus has been on me to retire for years, and I found a nice little place in Cabo where I can walk right out the front door and throw a line in the water."

Ember smiled. "That sounds nice, all right. You've certainly earned your retirement."

They parted ways and Ember returned to the house. She found Cedric and Reddy standing around, looking grim.

Ember's smile faded. She feared they'd had a row while she was outside with the mayor. She didn't want to disturb their tenuous peace, but her curiosity demanded she speak.

"What's wrong?" she looked between the two of them. "Did you have a fight?"

"No, Deputy McNair," Reddy said with exaggerated politeness. "We didn't have a fight."

"Then how come you both look so upset?

Cedric turned to her and sighed. "Smothers was about to lock up the station for the night when the call came in. Another body's been found."

TWENTY-TWO

Cedric glanced over at Ember as she tugged at the collar of her uniform shirt.

"How's it feel?"

Ember grimaced. "Scratchy and stiff. At least we found all the pins—I think."

Cedric chuckled, his blue eyes merry with delight. "I mean, how does it feel to be an official Deputy?"

"Weird," she said. "Quite frankly. I mean, what does this mean? Do I have to run from the Pub if there's an emergency? Are you my boss?"

"It's a formality so you can be present at crime scenes, interrogations, and the like," Cedric replied. "Don't stress about it. Just collect your salary and go on. You don't even have to wear the uniform when Reddy's—"

"Whoa, did you just say salary?"

"As a Deputy you draw a salary of twelve K per year."

"That—isn't this nepotism?"

"No," Cedric said firmly. "It's not nepotism. It's Caucherie, and, after all you've done to protect not only this town, but the very fabric of existence itself, twelve thousand a year is, literally, the least we can do."

Ember felt a glow in her chest, but she narrowed her gaze at Cedric. "I thought you couldn't remember all the times I helped before your amnesia."

"True, but I've been reading through my old case files," Cedric said. "You're mentioned. A lot. Apparently, I even thought you were a suspect at one point."

Ember chuckled. "I remember that. You tried so hard to pretend you didn't like me. At the beginning."

"I should have known that was a futile proposition." Cedric's grin faded as they turned onto the highway. "Have you ever been out to the Mussels' place before?"

Ember grew somber, shaking her head. "No. We don't travel in the same circles. Isn't he some kind of horse rancher?"

Cedric snorted in derision. "He wishes. More like a wealthy hobbyist."

They turned off the highway and took a long, private drive. They passed a sign which read *Mussels Ranch* as they approached a sprawling modern home with three stories and twice as many trucks parked out front.

The moonlight reflected off the trucks' windshields as they parked the squad car and met up with Agent Reddy. The three of them moved up the short sidewalk. Cedric rapped on the door.

A moment later, a graying woman with pretty, but tear-streaked, eyes appeared at the door. She clutched a wadded-up Kleenex in a hand before her chest. Her haunted eyes made Ember's heart swell with pity.

"Mrs. Mussels?" Cedric asked. "We came as soon as we could."

She looked at Cedric for a long moment before finding the ability to speak.

"H-he's out back," she said in a voice thick with grief. They followed Mrs. Mussels onto her back porch, where she lingered. She leaned against a support post and gestured vaguely at the back yard. "I found him...I found him out by the horse barn."

Reddy looked up at the outdoor lights hanging on wooden poles overhead. "Mrs. Mussels, would it be possible to get these lights turned on?"

She nodded, and silently padded into the house. Ember followed Cedric down the short flight of steps to the hard-packed dirt of their fenced-in horse corral. They approached the barn, their way lit only by moonlight. Ember couldn't make out anything which might be Mussels' body.

The light snapped on with a loud pop, flooding the backyard with light. Ember gasped at the sight of the rotund Buford Mussels, laying face down. The blue gingham check of his shirt and the shiny spurs on his boots seemed utterly at odds with his grim condition.

Ember looked about in the well-trod horse corral. The dirt had been hard-packed and wasn't likely to hold any prints, which she felt was a pity. With reluctance, she moved her eyes to the dead body.

Ember hadn't known Buford Mussels well. On, maybe, one occasion, he'd stopped in the Pub for a late lunch. Other than that, she knew him by reputation only. Most folks said he was cheerful enough but preferred to spend most of his time either working with his horses or talking people's ear off about them.

Cedric crouched down and pulled Buford's belt down.

He shook his head at the sight of the twin holes. "Same thing."

Reddy stared at Mussels for a long time, his jaw working silently. He glanced over at Ember and shook his head as if in contempt. Ember sneered at him and then turned back to examine the body.

She didn't detect the presence of magic, as with the last two bodies. Ember knew why Reddy was so contemptuous. Maybe she even deserved it.

Buford Mussels was a wealthy man, who was living his life's dream with his horse ranch even if he'd yet to generate any winners. His marriage was stable and happy, and he'd seen his adult children away to Ivy League universities.

In short, he was a happy man. Wednesdays' Child was supposed to be full of woe. Buford Mussels was about as far as you could get from woeful feelings.

Cedric looked over at Reddy. "What do you think, R.U.?"

Reddy shrugged. "I think your Deputy-wife is right. We've got a serial killer on our hands, and he's using that dumb nursery rhyme as his inspiration."

Ember flinched. "What? But...but Buford Mussels had a happy life. He's not full of woe."

Reddy pointed at the horse barn. "The man loved riding his horses. He was even stepping out for an evening ride when our killer reached him. He's full of woah, all right."

Reddy pantomimed pulling back on a set of reins.

Ember felt a surge of satisfaction that Reddy finally took her theory seriously. One look at the dead man at her feet was enough to remind her, being right in this case wasn't a good thing.

Not in the least.

TWENTY-THREE

mber's dreams were troubled that night. She couldn't recall their content but awakened several times in a sheen of sweat.

Cedric certainly hadn't helped her mood before bedtime. He'd studiously avoided being anywhere near her until she'd already gone to bed, as if afraid they might do something marital again.

Ember tried to tell herself to have patience, but it grew harder each and every day.

The next day she awoke to find Cedric and April already gone. He'd dropped her off early at school for a field trip to the city museum. Ember puttered around the house, mulling over her many problems.

She stood in front of the urn containing Cedric's memories for a long time. If all it took was force of will, she'd have already put his memories back in his head. Alas, she could do nothing but stare at the urn and hope fervently she could someday succeed in her goal.

"I want my husband back," she muttered to the urn.

Not for the first time, she cursed the name of the Glawkus and the Swamp Witch who'd summoned it.

Ember made it into the restaurant a little late, but found Ash and Willow had things well in hand. Her eyes nearly bulged out of her head when a wizened woman in a black dress and white apron came out of the kitchen holding a pitcher of iced tea.

"Meredith?" Ember blurted. "What are you doing in my kitchen?"

Meredith paled, then glanced over at Ash with a desperate light in her eyes.

Ash stepped forward quickly. "I hired her, it's all right."

"You hired her?" Ember stammered. "B-but...it's Meredith!"

"Yes, it is. Who else is going to work for minimum wage?"

Ember grabbed Ash's arm and dragged her into the kitchen. "Are you out of your mind? Meredith is a Dark Witch! She's caused us headaches aplenty over the years."

"Yes, she is, and she also loaned us the grimoire which helped us figure out how to find Cedric's memories, remember?" Ash sighed. "Meredith is on the outs with the dark coven in town, all right? The Ravens think she's too weak, and they're right. She can barely channel enough energy for the most minor cantrips."

"Unless she uses Dark Magic."

Ash sighed. "That's the other reason they kicked her out. Meredith has sworn off dark magic."

Ember frowned. "Why?"

"I think she got scared. She messed with something, a demon maybe, that drove her to swear it off for good. Look, she's alone, miserable, and she needs the work. Her social security check barely covers her utility bills."

Ember sighed. "All right, fine. But if she casts so much as a Dark cantrip she's out the door."

"Fair enough."

Ember puttered around the kitchen some, but, between Ash, Willow, and Meredith, there wasn't much for her to do. She eventually gathered up Kali, said her farewells, and went to the station house.

Ember and Cedric chatted with Reddy while they waited for Doc Dalton to finish his examination of Buford Mussels. Reddy's attitude toward Ember had changed one hundred and eighty degrees. She was glad of it, but felt Reddy should have given her such respect from the beginning.

"What did your tech boys say about the video posted to the town's Facebook page?" Cedric asked.

Reddy grimaced with disgust. "I didn't follow much of the actual words they used, but basically they can't help us. The guy used a turnip router or something."

"Onion router," Ember said.

"Yeah, that's the one. He covered his cyber tracks well enough it's a dead end."

Cedric's phone rang. He looked up after answering, his brows arched.

"Dalton's ready for us. Let's go see what he's found out."

They headed out to the new morgue. Doc Dalton stood between the bodies of Grace Fuller and Buford Mussels, scribbling down a note on his clipboard.

"What's the sitch, Doc?" Cedric asked. "Don't keep us in suspense."

Dalton set his clipboard down and gestured at Grace Fuller's body. "Well, both Fuller and Mussels died the same way as Olberman. Cardiac arrest caused by inundation with electricity."

Dalton picked up the taser gun Cedric had ordered and held the prongs out over the wounds on Mussel's back. It was a perfect fit. "This looks like a good match to our murder weapon. It's set up to continue to deliver shocks every time you squeeze the trigger."

"I thought this was a non-lethal weapon," Ember said.

"Less lethal, not non-lethal. Non-lethal is a misnomer." Dalton showed them the gun. "There's a regulator that prevents you from delivering more than a half-dozen shocks or so, to prevent cardiac arrest. But watch this."

He gave a twist of his fingers, and a piece snapped off the gun. "Just like that, you can remove the governor and zap someone until you run out of battery juice."

"It's not easy to get one of these," Cedric said. "I'll put Smothers on going through our suspects to see who might have been able to acquire one."

Ember snorted. "I can think of one man who could pull it off, legally or illegally."

"Whitman?" Cedric arched his brow.

"Whitman."

"I'll get a search warrant for his financial records going," Reddy said. "I've got a district judge on speed dial."

"Thanks," Cedric said with a nod.

"I found some additional forensic evidence on Miss Fuller's body."

They turned back to face Doc Dalton, whose red face seemed to indicate he felt uncomfortable.

"What's that, Doc?" Cedric asked.

"I found some human hair on her. Dark brown, definitely not her own. There was also some, ah...genetic material, if you catch my meaning."

Cedric nodded. "Good work, Doc."

"We'll run the DNA through the FBI database," Reddy said. "See if we get lucky."

Ember looked at the two bodies, her expression grim. Some luck would be nice, before yet another body found its way into the city morgue.

TWENTY-FOUR

Ember stopped by the Pub to see if she was needed for the lunch rush. She found Willow and Ash in the kitchen, nibbling on the rich meat gleaned from baking ham hocks.

"Those are for the baked beans," Ember said with a smile even as she popped a salty morsel into her own mouth. Willow offered Kali a piece, but the cat turned her nose up at it.

"Yuck, too salty," Kali said. "How about some Tender Vittles?"

Ember got the treat box off the high shelf and distributed several onto the counter for Kali to greedily crunch in her teeth.

"Hey, how's our newest deputy doing?" Ash looked Ember up and down. "You make that uniform look good, by the way."

"Oh stop, I look terrible in brown."

"Not true. It makes your butt look cute. Right, Willow?"

Willow let out a girlish giggle as Ember blushed. "Okay,

that's enough of that. Would you like to hear the latest in the investigation?"

"They're right. Your butt looks great in deputy pants," Kali said.

Ember led Ash off into the office, as she wasn't sure how much of what they said might travel from Willow's lips. Ember's jaw gaped open when she saw her office's condition. "W-what did you do to my office?"

Ash grunted in disdain. "Ugh. I cleaned it."

"How could you? Where is everything? I had a system, you know."

"What system? Total chaos?"

Ember opened the drawers of her filing cabinet and found that her invoices and receipts had been separated and organized. She realized Ash had gone to a lot of work, but it still felt like a violation.

"Hey, I'm sorry," Ash said, picking up on her mood. "I guess I should have asked."

"No, it's fine," Ember said, shaking her head in an effort to shake out the bad feelings. "It needed to be done. It's just...different."

"Different isn't always bad." Ash put a hand on Ember's shoulder. "How are you doing? You seem pretty stressed."

"I am stressed." Ember sighed. She told Ash about her night of passion with Cedric, and his subsequent withdrawal.

"You know what I think?" Ash asked. "We need a girl's night out. No men, just estrogen, baby. Get away from all of this murder and memories and mayhem."

"I don't know. It seems irresponsible somehow. Shouldn't we be researching spell creation if we have time to spare?"

"Ember, you've got to take care of your mental health.

Spell creation is very tricky, and we need you at one-hundred percent if we're even going to consider it. Trust me. Take the night off. Call Sage, see if she wants to go. Heck, we'll get Kathy in on this, even."

Ember heaved a sigh, then smiled at Ash. "Where do you want to go?"

"Yay!" Ash clapped her hands eagerly. "That's the spirit."

"You didn't answer my question."

"Oh, you should know the answer. The Big Easy is only an hour away."

"I'm not looking to wake up in a puddle of my own vomit," Ember said.

"Stop thinking about the worst that could happen," Ash said with an exasperated groan. "You've been so grumpy ever since Cedric's amnesia. That needs to stop."

"Grumpy?" Ember growled. "I'm not grumpy. What's your problem, anyway? Why do you always..."

Her voice trailed off as Ash arched an eyebrow. "Okay, so I guess I am kind of grumpy."

"We'll take care of that with some margaritas," Ash said. "There's this one bar called Charlie's that has THE hottest bartender."

Ember laughed at Ash's enthusiasm. "Fine for you, but I'm a married woman."

Ash laughed. "Just because you're on a diet, doesn't mean you can't look at the menu? And you're going to want to read this menu, I guarantee it."

Ember headed home to change and ask Cedric to watch April. He seemed almost relieved she would be out of the house. Given his avoidance of her ever since their passionate night, maybe he was relieved.

Ember slipped into a cute, but not slutty, sleeveless

black dress and modest heels, since she knew they'd be doing a lot of walking. Ash loved her pub crawls.

It turned out Sage was on board for a girls' night out, but Kathy begged off. Willow was foisted upon them, however.

"How are we going to get her into the bar? She's only eighteen, and you have to be twenty-one in most places."

Ash held up a piece of white plastic. "With this."

Ember stared at the chip of plastic, then recognized the glamour upon it. "You magicked up a fake ID for Willow? Are you out of your mind?"

"We don't have to let her drink, but this way she can at least come inside."

"You realize my husband is the sheriff, right? And I'm a deputy?"

"Yeah, are you going to arrest me?"

Ember laughed. "No, I guess not. It's fine, so long as she doesn't drink."

The drive to New Orleans was rife with raunchy comments and uproarious laughter. Ember's ribcage ached from the constant mirth. By the time they reached the city, they were already in a state.

Ember tried to be restrained, but by the third pub her vision blurred a bit, and it was hard to keep walking in a straight line.

"You're hammered," Ash said.

"You are, too," Ember pointed out.

Sage sighed. "Good thing I'm here to play chaperone."

"You've been drinking just as much as us. Willow is the chaperone."

Willow looked abashed, and Sage laughed.

"You're off the hook, sweetie." Sage leaned over and whispered in Ember's ear. "We shifters have a hartier constitution than most mortals. I'm not nearly as think as you drunk I am."

Ember frowned. Something about that sentence didn't seem right...

They made it to the next bar, settling around a table and ordering greasy bar food to absorb the alcohol in their bellies. Ash glanced over at Willow.

"Hey," she said around a mouthful of mozzarella stick. "How come your mom couldn't make it, again? Is she sick?"

Willow shook her head as she dipped a fried wing in hot sauce. "No, she was afraid of cheating on her diet. She's running in the New Orleans Half Marathon next month."

"How long's a half marathon?" Ash asked.

"Like thirteen miles, I think."

"Whew," Ash said. "Sounds like Kathy's got far to go before she hits the finish line."

Ember frowned, her brow furrowing with thought. Far to go...where had she heard that recently? Her beer-soaked brain struggled to make the connection.

Far to go...far to go...Wednesday's child has far to go...

Ember stood up so suddenly she knocked her chair over.

"We have to call Kathy," Ember said. "Now!"

TWENTY-FIVE

Ember stepped over a fallen log in the darkened wood, cupping her hands to her mouth.

"Kathy!" She called out strongly. "Kathy O'Connell!"

After Ember's frantic urging, Willow had called Kathy, and gotten no response. Ember tried on her phone, as did Sage. The results were the same.

They'd raced back to Caucherie, the sober Willow driving. On the way home, Ember and Ash used a charm to help sober up faster. By the time they made it home, they were clear headed enough to speak coherently with Cedric.

Cedric had immediately formed a search party, and they set to work. Kathy's car was found outside her café. Cedric suggested they begin the search in the woods out back. Ember was so eager to start the search, she still wore her black dress, though she'd put on her Deputy shoes in lieu of the heels.

"Kathy!" Ember called again. She moved through the darkened wood in a line with the other searchers. She heard

Sharon and Mark Dalton calling for Kathy, along with a chorus of other voices.

A black, winged shape darted through the woods and disappeared behind a bush. A moment later Sage emerged from the underbrush, panting and out of breath.

"I flew all the way to the river and back, and I saw no sign of her."

"Sage, you're exhausted. Take a break."

Sage shook her head. "Can't you narrow the search down with magic?"

Ember sighed. "I wish I could. Locator magics are among the trickiest because the spirits you deal with have such a hard time comprehending corporeal existence."

"Then I guess I'm doing this the hard way. I'll take another trip to the river, and fade east this time."

"Sage, wait!" Ember cried. Sage leaped into the air, transforming in the blink of an eye into a winged bat. She veered through the darkened woods and disappeared.

The search party made it to the river an hour later, disillusioned when they hadn't seen a trace of the missing wife and mother.

Cedric set his party to walking along the river, just in case they spotted something. Then he called Ember over to his side.

"I don't think we can do much more good out here tonight," he said. Cedric checked his phone. "Or should I say, this morning. You should go home and get some sleep."

"No," Ember said, shaking her head firmly. "Not until we find Kathy."

"Ember..." Cedric sighed.

"I'm not stopping until we find her," Ember repeated firmly.

Cedric's lips became a thin, tight line. She could see

him weighing his options in his blue eyes. At length he nodded. "All right. Want to come with me to Chad Whitman's and collect hair and DNA samples?"

Ember nodded. "Yes, I do."

Despite her bravado, Ember fought the urge to drift off to sleep during the drive out to Chad Whitman's compound. Every time she let her eyes close, it felt like a betrayal of Kathy and their friendship. She wound up clenching her fists tight enough that her nails dug into the palms of her hands. It helped, some.

They reached Chad's compound gate just after dawn. Cedric honked his squawking horn, then hit the sirens until Chad appeared at his door, holding a rifle in his hands.

Chad saw it was the sheriff and rolled his eyes. He set the gun down and came to the gate, dressed only in boxer shorts and a pair of flip flops.

"What are you doing here? It's six in the morning!"

"I'm here to serve you warrants, Mr. Whitman," Cedric said. He handed the papers through the cyclonic fence and Whitman squinted at them.

"Oh, you want my hair, and my DNA?" Whitman rifled through the crinkling papers and laughed. "You must have found something on Gracie, right? Well, I used her services a few times, so I'm not surprised."

Cedric scowled. Ember fought down the urge to growl like an animal. Chad had just neatly accounted for any of his physical evidence that might match that found on Fuller's body.

"There's one more warrant, Whitman. I wouldn't gloat so soon."

Whitman turned white. "You—you're going to search my property?"

He stared at the warrant, eyes narrowed to slits. Whitman's face changed, turning red with anger.

"This—this is outrageous! You're going to search my financial records? For what reason?"

"Call your lawyer, have him explain it to you," Cedric said. He extracted a thin plastic cup from a leather zippered bag. "Now, open wide. I need to swab your cheek. Fortunately, we can do it through your fence."

Whitman opened his mouth, glaring at Cedric as he took a sample. He even allowed Cedric to use a tiny pair of tweezers to pluck out a few strands of hair.

Whitman seemed far angrier about his finances being put on display. "I knew it, you can't get me for any of your trumped-up charges, so you're going to sic the IRS on me. You're a real piece of work, Sherriff."

"Have a nice day, Mr. Whitman," Cedric said. He and Ember strode back to the squad car. Ember cast a glance over her shoulder.

"Is it just me, or was he terrified of us searching his property?"

"I'm sure he's got some illegally modified weapons somewhere he didn't want us to see," Cedric said with a shrug. His eyes seemed haunted as he turned on the engine.

"What's wrong?"

"I have to go to my oldest friend and take his DNA," Cedric said. "I really hope Hanky-Bob's clean. If he's not..."

Ember set her jaw hard. If Hanky-Bob were guilty, it would destroy Cedric. For her husband's sake, she hoped Hanky-Bob didn't have anything to hide.

TWENTY-SIX

"I don't understand," Ember said as they drove past Caucherie's city limits. "How did Hanky-Bob even wind up on the FBI's DNA database, anyway?"

"He didn't." Cedric barely opened his clenched jaw to speak. His eyes bored holes into the path ahead. "Reddy snatched a beer bottle Hanky-Bob had been drinking from and sealed it in a plastic bag."

"Reddy really has it in for Hanky-Bob, doesn't he?" Ember shook her head. "All over a stupid car."

Cedric grunted as he flicked his sun visor down. Ember did the same, but her shorter stature meant her visor was largely ineffectual. She grimaced in annoyance until they turned a curve and the early morning sun no longer blinded her.

"Truth to tell, the car was just the match. Reddy and Hanky-Bob never got along, not really. Kind of like putting Bill O'Reilly in the same room as Michael Moore, if you catch my drift."

"I just hope Reddy can be professional, and not take out his grudge on Hanky-Bob."

Gravel rocks popped as they turned down Hanky-Bob's driveway. They found the mechanic working on a primer-covered corvette, surrounded by several of his friends. Cedric smiled genially at them as they approached.

"Hey Sheriff," said a balding man whose confederate flag T-shirt hung so long it covered up most of his denim shorts. His eyes fell on Ember and a sly grin came to his beard-stubbled face. "Hey, why didn't you tell me you hired a new deputy? How you doin' gorgeous?"

Cedric's eyes narrowed. Ember felt a surge of magic from him. Was he really so angry he was about to shift forms in front of mundane witnesses?

Ember swiftly removed her hat, allowing her long hair to tumble down. "I'm married, that's how I am, Cleetus."

Cleetus's face went pale. "Oh crap, I'm sorry. I didn't recognize you with the uniform, and...um...."

Cedric continued to stare down Cleetus until he retreated a short distance away. Hanky-Bob had extricated himself from under the car and rose to his feet with a helping hand from one of his buddies.

"Sheriff," Hanky-Bob said with stiff formality. Ember felt a stab of pathos in her chest. Cedric's job hurt his friendships at times, and this was one of them.

"Hanky-Bob," Cedric said, taking off his shades and folding them neatly before stuffing them in his pocket. "Is there somewhere we can talk? Privately?"

Hanky-Bob glanced over at his friends and spoke with exaggerated casualness. "Jeb, see if you can get that dang muffler off. Use a carbon saw if you have to, thing's rusted on tighter than a gator's jaws."

Hanky-Bob moved with resigned dread as he led them to his front porch some fifty feet from the garage. He turned to Cedric as soon as the screen door banged shut behind them.

"What's this about?"

Cedric sighed. "Hanky-Bob, I'm going to level with you. Things aren't looking good for you right now. If there's anything you want to tell me, particularly about the night Gracie died, now is the time."

Hanky-Bob sat down heavily on a wrought iron chair, the striped cushion disappearing beneath his bulk. He didn't look at them when he spoke.

"Oh, come on, Cedric. I—I've been lonely since Becky left, all right?" He half-laughed. "The funny thing is, she only came over because her rice burner had a sticky clutch. We got to talking, and, well, I realized she wasn't a sleaze, or a skank. She was just a woman trying to do the best she could for herself and her kid."

Ember gasped. "Fuller had a child?"

"Fuller's grandmother has custody. They live a couple towns over." Cedric fixed Hanky-Bob with a stern gaze. "So, what happened after that? Did you fix her clutch?"

"Yeah, it was easy. Took maybe twenty minutes." Hanky-Bob sighed. "It was so easy and didn't even require parts other than a couple of bolts, so I told her it was on the house. She, um, said she didn't want to owe me anything, and suggested...something else."

Cedric nodded. "So, you slept with her?"

Hanky-Bob hid his face in his hands and nodded.

"What time did Gracie leave, Hanky-Bob?" Ember asked.

He pulled his hands away from his face and looked thoughtful. "Around eight. Sun was just going down."

"And she drove her car home?"

Hanky-Bob shrugged. "I don't know where she was

headed, but yeah, the car was in good shape, all things considered."

Cedric nodded, scribbling something on a pad. He motioned Ember over to the end of the porch and spoke in a low voice.

"We found Gracie's car parked outside her trailer."

"That supports what Hanky-Bob is telling us, doesn't it."

Cedric looked grim. "Gracie was five-feet, four-inches tall. When Smothers found the car, he noted the seat was all the way back. Far enough for a large man."

Ember cringed. Cedric walked back to Hanky-Bob and looked down at him sadly.

"What's up, Cedric?" Hanky-Bob said anxiously. "What's that look for?"

"Hanky-Bob, I'm really sorry about this." He sighed. "I'm placing you under arrest."

Hanky-Bob's jaw went slack. The profound hurt in his eyes was enough to make Ember want to cry. A moment later, his face turned red, and he leaped to his feet.

"You want to arrest me? Fine." Hanky-Bob turned around and put his hands behind his back. "Go ahead, arrest me. There's a folding knife in my right pocket and a screwdriver in my left, so don't poke yourself."

Cedric sighed. "I'm not going to cuff you, Bob. Come on, let's go."

Cedric gently guided his friend toward the waiting squad car. Ember's heart broke just a little, but she resolved to clear Hanky-Bob's name.

Her gut told her Bob was innocent, but she knew she had to prepare herself for the possibility he was not.

It could be true. Cedric's oldest friend might be a killer.

TWENTY-SEVEN

Cedric, Ember, and Hanky-Bob joylessly entered the station house to find Agent Reddy ensconced behind the desk.

Reddy stood up and glared first at Bob, then Cedric. "Why is this prisoner not in handcuffs?"

Cedric glared at Reddy. "Because he's not resisting. I'm taking him to a holding cell right now."

"No," Reddy said. "Take him to the interrogation room."

"What?" Cedric shook his head. "He needs to call his lawyer first."

"Put him in the room, Sheriff. I'm not going to ask twice. Don't worry, I'll take good care of Hanky-Bob until his legal counsel arrives."

Cedric sighed. He and Ember took Hanky-Bob to the interrogation room. "Don't tell him anything until your lawyer gets here, Hanky-Bob. You have the right to remain silent."

"Yeah, yeah, don't act like you give a crap, Cedric."

Hanky-Bob plopped down in the chair. "You want to help, go catch the guy who actually killed Gracie."

Cedric closed the door and made a beeline for Reddy. "I want to be there when you talk to him."

"Not a chance, Slick Ric," Reddy said, shaking his head. "Everyone knows you and him are tight. We can't have you bringing your personal bias into the interrogation."

"Look who's talking!" Ember said, her sharp tone lingering in the air. "You've already convicted him in your head."

Reddy opened his eyes wide, brows climbing high on his forehead. "Oh, is that so? I admit, I like him for this. I like him a lot."

"Why?"

Reddy ticked off his points on his fingers. "One, he was the last person we know of to see our vic alive. Two, his DNA was found in her body. Three, the car we found had its seat pulled all the way back. We all know Ms. Fuller's feet could never have reached."

Cedric sighed. "Okay, fine, that connects him to Gracie in a purely circumstantial way, I might add. But what about the other murders?"

"Hanky-Bob openly stated his hatred for Olberman in front of multiple witnesses. As far as Mussels goes, I don't pretend to understand the workings of diseased minds."

"Come on, R.U.," Cedric said with exasperation. "Even you've got to admit that's a stretch."

Reddy reached over and snatched a sheaf of papers off the front desk. He shoved them against Cedric's chest.

"Hanky-Bob's financial records. Read it and weep. He purchased the same software program used to create our CGI Jester a couple of months ago."

Cedric frowned. "He was trying to use it to make a

video for his business and post it on his social media pages. He told me all about it."

"Sounds like he was trying to establish an alibi to me." Reddy sighed. "Look, Ric, you did your job, and did it well. You and your Deputy Wife. But now it's time to step back and let me do mine, you feel me?"

Cedric grabbed a sheaf of papers off the desk and stalked toward his office. Ember followed after a moment's hesitation. She closed the door behind them as Reddy went off to the interrogation room.

"What's that?" Ember asked.

"Chad Whitman's financial records and background check." Cedric handed her half the stack of papers. "Can you do financial, while I go over his background?"

"Sure thing." They poured over their respective pages for nearly an hour, sometimes taking notes or remarking on things to each other. When they finished, Ember summed up her findings.

"No record of him purchasing the taser gun, or the CGI software. I did find something that may help us, though."

"What's that?"

"His water and electricity bills are twice as high as when he first moved to the property. He might have a grow going there."

Cedric arched his brows. "You think he's growing pot? Maybe. It would explain why he didn't want us to search his property, and where he gets all the money to fund his private arsenal on a blogger's income."

"Can we get a search warrant?"

"Maybe. It'll be hard to get a judge to sign off on just the utility bills, but maybe."

Ember sighed. "What did you find?"

"Reddy was right, much as I hate to admit it. Chad

Whitman is clean as a whistle. His only legal trouble was sending the threatening letters. He was investigated for a lot of crimes in his twenties, but never got formally charged."

"Why not?" Ember said, her suspicions inflamed.

"Well, in most of the cases he turned out to have a rock-solid alibi, even when eyewitnesses put him at the scene of the crime." Cedric shrugged. "For the most part, he's a law-abiding citizen, at least according to his records."

Ember rubbed her temples. "That makes it less likely a judge will sign off on a search warrant. You know, I could grab my broom and do a fly-over of his compound. Maybe take some photos—"

"That won't be admissible in court."

"No, but it might give us enough for a search warrant of his property."

Cedric grew silent. He mulled over her idea for a long moment and then shook his head. "How would we explain where the photos came from?"

Ember sighed. "Well..."

She gasped, eyes shining with eager light. "Oh, I know. We'll tell them they were drone photos taken during an ecological survey."

Cedric stared at her for a long moment before his face split in a wide grin. "All right. Where's your broom?"

"In the trunk of my car, I think. Let me go check."

Ember and Cedric left the office and went to the building's exit. Before they could open it, the front door swung wide and a pear-shaped, balding man in a suit entered the station house.

"Greetings, Sheriff," he said with an exaggerated, stiff formality. "My name is Heywood Paulson, and I represent Chad Whitman."

"You're Whitman's lawyer?" Cedric cocked his head to the side. "What do you want?"

"I have something you have to see. Once you've seen it," Paulson's eyes glittered with delight "you won't even think about charging my client for the murder of Grace Fuller."

TWENTY-EIGHT

Heywood Paulson placed his leather briefcase on the front desk and unsnapped the brass fastenings with precise clicks. With a flourish, he opened the case and produced a VHS cassette tape for their inspection.

"Lady and Gentlemen, what I hold before you is a monumental piece of evidence. This humble VHS tape was once ensconced in the manager's office of the Creole Corner convenience store near the interstate exit. You might be wondering what it was—"

"Get on with it, Paulson," Reddy snapped. "You're not in court, and there's no jury to impress."

Paulson's eyes narrowed in a glare. He cleared his throat gruffly and continued.

"This VHS tape is the security footage from a particular evening of great import. The very same evening that Ms. Fuller expired."

"Was murdered," Cedric corrected.

"Be that as it may, once you see this footage you will not consider my client to be a suspect."

Cedric frowned. "I don't think we have a VCR in the station."

"Shoot, can you even buy them anymore?" Reddy asked.

"I've got a VCR, sir," Smothers said.

Reddy chuckled. "Good job, Deputy. Your porn collection is going to be of use to us."

Smothers glared at him. "Actually, I belong to the Tape Heritage Project. We're trying to transfer as many VHS tapes to digital storage as we can before they can no longer be played. It's important for history."

Reddy cleared his throat. "Ah, well now...could you get that VCR for us, Deputy?"

"I can, if you apologize for insulting me."

Ember hid a laugh as Reddy stewed. Cedric turned to Reddy and cocked an eyebrow, as if to say 'well, we're waiting.' Even Paulson seemed to enjoy the way Reddy squirmed.

"Deputy Smothers, I humbly apologize for impugning your character, even in jest. Would you please retrieve your VCR?"

Smothers stood up. "Certainly."

In short order, they ensconced themselves in Cedric's office. There was some fumbling to get the VCR display on the monitor screen, but thanks to Smothers they got it squared away.

A grainy, black and white image appeared on screen. Actually, Ember realized it was four images of different spots inside of a typical gas station food mart.

"I've taken the liberty of fast forwarding through the first two hours to the pertinent time frame," Paulson said. "You'll notice my client enters the store at nine-thirty."

"What's the point of this, Mr. Paulson?" Cedric asked

with an impatient snort. "The time of death for our victim is around eleven to midnight. Whitman would have had plenty of time to—"

"Just keep watching."

Whitman entered the convenience store, hands thrust in his pockets as he wandered over to the magazine rack. He picked up a Field and Stream and thumbed through it.

"Not all of the cameras have audio. Only the one at the counter by the register," Paulson said. "But watch this."

Another man came and stared at the magazine rack as well. Whitman turned and spoke with him genially. Ember couldn't hear what was said, but the two men shook hands and continued to speak.

"We can fast forward here," Paulson said. "For the next thirty minutes, my client spoke with this man—a local of good repute—about bass fishing."

They watched the tape for over an hour, Heywood occasionally fast forwarding. The entire time, Whitman never left the store. In fact, he never even left sight of any of the cameras, not even for a moment.

Whitman drank coffee, spoke to the clerk, spoke to nearly everyone who came in the door. He purchased snacks and cigarettes, messed around on his phone, and generally just hung out in the convenience store until well after one in the morning.

"Given the time of death, Sheriff, I'd appreciate it if you made a formal statement that my client was no longer a person of interest in this case."

Reddy chuckled without mirth. "That Whitman's a loud-mouthed son of a gun, and, personally, I'd never crack open a cold one with him, but...let's face it, Ric. He's clean."

Ember shook her head. "This doesn't make sense. Whitman hates people. He never leaves his compound unless he has to. Why is he acting like Mr. Social Butterfly?"

"Perhaps you don't know my client as well as you might think, Deputy," Paulson said smugly. "I'll leave this footage in your capable hands. Good day, gentlemen, Lady."

Ember watched as Heywood waddled out of the office. "What a slime puppy."

"He's a lawyer," Reddy said with a shrug, as if that explained everything. "But unfortunately, he's also not wrong. That gives Whitman an alibi."

"I agree with Ember that it's out of character for Whitman, but..." he sighed. "It does exonerate him."

"If Whitman's not our guy, then who is?" Ember asked.

Reddy snickered. "He's sitting in your interrogation room right now."

"I just don't think Hanky-Bob could kill someone."

Reddy fixed Ember with a stern gaze. "Deputy Wife Ember, you're sharp as a tack, and a natural born detective."

Ember flinched, not expecting a compliment. She sensed an imminent 'but', however.

"But you just haven't seen as much crap as I have in the FBI. I've seen wives happily married to their husbands for thirty years poison them for ten grand in insurance money. I've seen kids as young as twelve who try to burn their house down—with their family inside. The fact is, everybody's got a dark side. Whether we want to see it or not."

Ember covered her mouth with her hand and wrestled with Reddy's words as he and Cedric left the office. Everyone had a dark side...her recent struggles with the temptation to use Dark Magic rose up into her mind.

Maybe Hanky-Bob was a killer. If it were true, then the world was a much darker place than she'd ever imagined.

TWENTY-NINE

Feeling a need to be useful, Ember and Cedric rejoined the search party looking for Kathy. They drove to the other side of the river behind her café and picked up the search there.

"Do you really think she would have come across the river?" Willow asked, her eyes puffy with recent weeping.

"If she were trying to get away from someone or something, yes," Ember said.

"But it's been days. Wouldn't we have found her by now if she was...if she was..."

Willow sniffled until Cedric put his hand on her slender shoulder.

"Hey, now. When I was still a deputy, I worked a missing person case. Everyone expected foul play but, come to find out, the guy was lost on his own property. Just about two square miles. These woods are ten times that, so it's totally feasible your mother is out here somewhere."

That helped, a little. Willow moved off to join some of her relatives in a group hug. Ember and Cedric began moving carefully through the woods, calling Kathy's name from time to time.

"Have you tried going full-on wolf and picking up her scent?" Ember asked.

Cedric shook his head. "There's so much mold in the air this time of year it messes with my sinuses. I can barely detect your scent and you're a few feet away."

Ember sighed. "I just feel so helpless. I was so sure Chad Whitman had something to do with the murders, and now..."

"It's hard to argue with video evidence."

"I know, but Chad was acting so strange. Who hangs out at a convenience mart for five hours?"

"I agree it's strange and totally out of character for him. But there are dozens of eyewitnesses, including the clerk himself. It was definitely Chad Whitman and not a look-alike."

They continued the search until the sun kissed the horizon. Ember reminded Cedric they needed to pick up April soon.

They made the drive in somber silence. Ember wanted to say something to reassure Cedric but had no idea what. Words seemed so weak, so empty. How do you soothe a person whose best, oldest friend was facing murder charges —and a possible death sentence?

Ember put on a brave face for April and chatted with the girl on their way home. Cedric seemed lost in thought, his eyes distant as they traveled home.

She nudged Cedric when he put the car in park and turned the engine off but failed to get out. "Hey. Come on inside."

"Sorry," he said. "I'll help with dinner."

"Hmmm." Ember shook her head. "Let's get pizza

instead. Neither of us are in a state of mind where we want to cook."

"Pizza, yay!" April said, clapping her hands fiercely. "I want pineapples and ham."

"We'll get you your own," Ember said, trying to hide her disgust. In her estimation, pineapples on pizza were an abomination.

They had dinner in the living room, watching the Saints game on the television. Normally Cedric would hoot and holler at touchdowns, or moan in discontent with the fumbles. That night, he simply chewed his food in silence, watching the game with apparent disinterest.

After dinner, he went out onto the porch to brood. Ember settled April in with a streamed cartoon series and went to the fridge. She extracted two bottles of beer and pushed open the screen door with her shoulder.

Cedric looked up in surprise as she handed him a brew. Ember settled on the porch swing beside him. She picked up the tablet off a side table and clicked it to life.

"What's up?"

"We're a little behind on our bookkeeping. I thought we'd get bills paid and see if there's enough left over to get April horseback riding lessons."

"Oh. Okay." Cedric seemed at least somewhat relieved to have something else to think about. "Are we really spending that much on groceries?"

"Ever since April moved in we are."

"But she's only a little girl. She eats that much?"

"She's in a growth spurt, and, besides, we have to buy things you and I don't eat, like Halos and frozen French fries. Not only that, her shampoo, soap, toothpaste...there's a lot on the grocery bill besides food."

Cedric grunted. "It's not like money is a problem, with

your Deputy salary, my salary, and the income from the bar."

"Right. We're doing good, we just got busy and forgot to pay a couple of things. Pete from the power company called to give us a gentle reminder."

"How is Pete?"

"Doing well. He's still trying to sell that fishing boat of his."

Ember used the tablet to pay their electric bill. Cedric grimaced at the expense. "Four hundred dollars?"

"Three hundred sixty-eight. That's last month's bill, too."

"Our bill's barely been over a hundred dollars for months."

"True, but now we have April."

Cedric relaxed. "Oh, of course. Sorry. Don't mean to sound like a miser, it just seemed like a lot of money."

"It is a lot of money, but it's explainable. Having a whole other person in your house runs the bills up…"

Ember's eyes widened as she sucked in a sudden gasp of air. Cedric perked up immediately.

"What's wrong?" Cedric asked.

"We need to talk to Reddy," Ember said. "Now!"

THIRTY

Ember poured a cup of fragrant coffee at the Sheriff's station. Despite the late hour, she didn't feel tired. A giddy energy had seized hold of her, making the coffee almost redundant.

Cedric peered out the window and grunted softly. "Looks like Whitman and his lawyer are here."

"That means we're just waiting on Earl Kleen." Ember checked her phone. "I'm a little anxious that Reddy's not here yet."

"R.U. will pull through for us, don't worry. He'll be here."

Ember nodded as Heywood Paulson pushed the door open and sauntered up to the front desk. "You've got a lot of nerve calling my client up here in the middle of the night, Sheriff. This is starting to feel persecutory."

"So glad you could make it, Mr. Paulson," Cedric said with a cheerful grin. "Please, come this way. I'll show you to my office."

"If we're not out of here in an hour, my client and I are

leaving. You have no authority to hold him, and his presence here should be considered a courtesy."

Cedric grinned widely. "Of course. Right this way, please."

Whitman passed Ember by, giving her the smuggest grin she'd ever seen. Ember cocked an eyebrow, then found herself distracted by the arrival of Brian Kleen. Like Paulson, he arrived with a lawyer—three of them, in fact."

Kleen entered first, flanked by his legal team. Ember smiled at him. "Thanks for coming, Mr. Kleen."

"I'm always willing to help out law enforcement," he said. "Don't mind my lawyers. It's a habit I've developed. I don't think I need legal counsel at this point."

Ember smiled at his fishing statement and decided to let him wonder. "If you'll come this way, we'll get started."

Ember led Kleen and his legal team into Cedric's office. There weren't enough chairs, so Smothers brought in some folding ones. When everyone was settled, Smothers reappeared with Hanky-Bob.

"What's the meaning of this?" Paulson's eyes narrowed to slits. "Why is this criminal, this murderer, in our midst?"

"Sorry to interrupt your penchant for the theatrical," Cedric said. "But all will be made clear if you'll all just be patient."

Cedric turned his gaze to Ember. It took her a moment to realize it was her cue to begin. "Oh, you want me to...right."

Ember cleared her throat and looked around the people gathered in the room. "Thank you all for coming out here, despite the late hour."

"I wasn't up to much," Hanky-Bob quipped.

"I was," Whitman snapped. "Let's get this over with."

"All right." Ember picked up her tablet and displayed a still from the Jester video uploaded to the town's Facebook page. "We're here to settle the matter of, who is the Foolkiller?"

"Open and shut," Heywood said, pointing his finger at Hanky-Bob. "That guy. Can we go home now?"

"Not so fast." Ember gestured at Hanky-Bob. "It's true, Hanky-Bob had a physical relationship with one of our victims, but he's not the only one."

Heywood sneered. "I know what you're implying, and quite frankly it sickens me. My client has a rock-solid alibi."

Ember nodded toward Paulson. "We'll get to your client in a bit. Hanky-Bob also appears to be among the last people to see Grace Fuller alive. He also admitted to owning the CGI software that created the Foolkiller video."

"Because he is the Foolkiller," Heywood said.

Cedric scowled. "Mr. Paulson, I don't know how they do things up in New York, but down here in the south we listen to people when they speak, instead of interrupting them."

Paulson spread his hands out and looked somewhat abashed. Ember continued on.

"Not to mention, Hanky-Bob has been openly hostile toward Ron Olberman. Of course, he's not the only one to threaten people in this room."

"My client's previous record is not an issue here. Besides, he paid his debt to society by undergoing anger management training."

"Your client has a history of seething anger, as well as ways of accessing the taser gun used in the murders."

"You can order those tasers off the internet."

"True enough." Ember turned to Earl Kleen. "Out of anyone in this room, you perhaps had the strongest motivation for killing Ron Olberman."

"He was my father-in-law! How dare you—"

"Relax, I'm just making an observation. You stand to inherit his media and real estate empire by proxy, since your wife is his heir. And, like Hanky-Bob, you lack an alibi for any of the murders."

Ember looked around the room, winding up to a crescendo. "In short, all three of you have been suspected of this crime. One of you has even been charged. But only one of you is the Foolkiller who's been terrorizing this town."

"Perhaps you'd care to enlighten us as to who before midnight?" Paulson quipped.

Ember narrowed her gaze. "Very well, Mr. Paulson. Our killer is...right there."

She pointed her finger, and the room erupted in chaos.

THIRTY-ONE

"Outrageous!" Heywood Paulson leaped to his feet, standing almost protectively over his nervous-seeming client. "Mr. Whitman has done nothing but cooperate with this investigation from the get-go, and he has an alibi for the night of Grace Fuller's murder. On what grounds do you make these accusations?"

Ember looked him dead in the eye. "On the grounds the man in the convenience store video is not your client."

Paulson looked confused, then angry. "Preposterous. You saw the footage. Everyone agrees it's Whitman in the video. Everyone."

Ember cocked an eyebrow. "Oh, it's a Whitman all right. Just not the Whitman who's sitting here with us today."

Chad Whitman reached into his pocket and Cedric clamped a hand down on his wrist. For a tense moment it looked as if there were going to be a fight, but Cedric squeezed tighter and Chad's will to fight drained from his face. Cedric took the pistol out of his jacket.

"Just keep your hands where I can see them," Cedric warned. "Let the Deputy finish."

"Yes, let her finish." Paulson turned a glare on Ember. "I know she wouldn't make such a brazen accusation without proof."

A knock at Cedric's door made Ember smile. "Here's your proof right here."

She opened the door and R.U. Reddy entered the office. He nodded to Ember and handed her a manilla envelope.

"Thank you, Agent Reddy." Ember held the folder in the air. "Chad Whitman had a brother, the departed Kevin Whitman. But, as it turns out, he had another brother, one not found in public records because he was given up for adoption."

She opened the folder and held up several photos. Heyman scowled. "Those are photos of my client."

"No, they're not. They're photos of Blake Whitman, or, should I say, Blake Redding, since his adoptive parents changed his name. He's Chad's identical twin brother."

Heywood Paulson clammed up. He cast a dirty look at his client. "What's the deal, Chad? I told you I couldn't help you if you weren't totally honest."

"I—I don't know what they're talking about," Chad blurted. "I don't have a twin brother."

Ember tilted her head to the side and put her hand on her hip. She snapped her fingers and Reddy handed her a sheaf of paper.

"What I have here are the transcripts of text messages between Chad Whitman and Blake Redding, dated some ten years ago. In these texts, they not only discuss their familial connection, they scheme about being able to commit crimes and still have the perfect alibi."

Paulson's face turned red. "You lied to me, you son of a—"

"Calm down, Mr. Paulson," Cedric said. "Chad Whitman and his twin brother have been lying to a lot of people for a very long time. You're hardly the first to get the wool pulled over your eyes."

"So, I have a twin brother, so what?" Chad shrugged. "That doesn't prove it's not me on those videos instead of him."

Ember smiled smugly, enjoying the way Chad squirmed. "Is that so? Here, catch."

She grabbed a paperweight from Cedric's desk and tossed it at Chad. Whitman caught it out of the air and frowned. "What was that for?"

"Why did you catch that with your right hand?"

"Because I'm right-handed," Whitman said with a scowl. "What's the point of all of this?"

"And you text with your right hand, write with your right hand?"

"Duh. This is what happens when you give a woman authority. She starts thinking she's God's gift to everything."

"Uh huh," Ember said. She held up her tablet and played the video from the convenience store. "Everyone please note this section of the video, where Whitman fills out a lottery sheet. He uses his left hand."

She stared around the room. "Chad and Blake Whitman are virtually identical in appearance in every way, but with some key differences. Chad is right-handed, but his brother is left-handed. It's a common phenomenon with identical twins, who can also have different fingerprints and even DNA."

"I admit to nothing," Chad snapped. "You think any of this will hold up in court?"

"If it does, you'll have to find another lawyer," Paulson said. "I quit."

He stormed out of the office. Whitman sneered as he went.

"Good riddance. I don't need a scum-sucking lawyer, anyway. You'll see. I'm not going down for this."

"Excuse me," Kleen said. "I have to ask, why was I brought here at all if you didn't think I was the killer?"

Cedric cocked an eyebrow at him. "Because traffic camera footage shows your chauffeur opening the door of Fuller's Hyundai and putting her seat back. Tampering with evidence is a crime, Mr. Kleen."

Kleen's face went red. One of the lawyers stepped forward. "Mr. Kleen had nothing to do with any such thing. Perhaps one of his employees went rogue in a misguided attempt to protect his boss."

Cedric snorted. "Yeah, right. We'll have to see what the county prosecutor thinks of that explanation, won't we?"

Ember moved over to Chad and glared down at him. "Mr. Whitman, where is Kathy O'Conner?"

Whitman stiffened up. He snidely cocked his head to the side and said "Who's that?"

"I think you know who she is, and I think you know where she is." Ember's eyes narrowed to slits. "We've got enough to convict you, and you know it. You're staring down the barrel of a lethal injection."

Chad paled until he was whiter than the files in Ember's hand. "So, I'll make you a deal, Mr. Whitman. If you tell us where Kathy is, and she's still alive, I'll ask my husband to use his influence to get you life in prison, instead."

Chad sneered. "That's a crummy choice."

Ember glared at him. "Live or die, it's your choice."

Chad shrugged. "Maybe I'm okay with dying."

Ember fought the urge to strike him. He knew where Kathy was, she was sure of it.

"What tipped you off to the twin brother thing?" Hanky Bob asked with glee as Cedric removed his handcuffs.

"Whitman's power bills spiked recently, as did his water usage. It mirrored the effect of us having April move in. That was the eureka moment, but I confirmed it with Agent Reddy. Plus, there was Whitman's strange behavior at the convenience store."

"I want to know why," Cedric growled. "Why the Foolkiller?"

Chad laughed. "Because, if you're fighting the good fight and trying to save this country from the ravages of those who hate it, you have to do it in disguise. The wrong people die and, all of the sudden, every truth-telling social media personality is on a watch list. But you create a villain and let it take the heat, and they leave you alone."

"Why Olberman? Why any of them, for that matter?" Cedric asked.

Whitman sneered. "Olberman was a globalization proponent, and shipped jobs overseas to China. Mussels was an effete snob in the same mold. And, as for the whore, well...I think you can figure that part out."

Ember viciously slapped Chad across the cheek. She glared down at him, anger surging through her body. The lights overhead flickered and darkened, almost winking out entirely.

"Chad Whitman, you will tell me where Kathy O'Connell is, or I will devour your soul."

"The compound, the compound!" Whitman hollered. "She's at the compound! In the barn!"

"Ember." Cedric's hand rested on her shoulder. Ember

started at his touch. The lights came back on fully, and she blinked in confusion.

What came over me?

Ember rushed toward the door.

"Where are you going?" Cedric called.

"To rescue Kathy."

"Wait, don't go by yourself!"

Ember ran out to the parking lot. She cast a cantrip to pop her trunk open and leaped into the air. Her broom darted out of the open drunk and she landed astride its polished wood back. She rocketed into the night sky, silhouetted against the moon before vanishing into the darkness.

THIRTY-TWO

Ember's hair straightened out behind her like a brush as she tore through the humid Louisiana sky. She poured on the speed, hands gripping her broom tightly. Ember felt a light pop behind her and wasn't surprised to hear Kali's telepathic voice in her head.

"Are you trying to fly off into danger without your trusted familiar?"

Ember grinned in spite of her urgent purpose. "Not at all. I put the Familiar Pocket spell on the broom for a reason."

"Cedric's worried sick. Wants me to tell you to wait for him."

Ember snorted. "Well, let him worry, then. I can handle myself. Blake Whitman's not even a witch."

"I can't believe we all thought the Foolkiller was Hanky-Bob." Kali shifted behind Ember, adhered to the broom by magic as much as her claws.

"Well, he did lie to us, and slept with a prostitute. Things might have went better for him if he'd come clean."

"I still can't believe Chad's got a twin brother. Or that you figured it out looking at some bills."

"It wasn't just that. Cedric thought he heard someone moving around inside Chad's house, the weird behavior on the convenience store video, and all of the perfectly-timed alibis for the dozens of crimes Chad had been accused of in his twenties. It all culminated in that moment."

"It's still impressive." Kali shifted about nervously. Ember could detect the anxiety in her mind when Kali 'spoke' next. "Do you think Kathy is still alive?"

Ember cringed. Her heart broke at the thought of having to tell Willow that her mother was dead.

"I hope so. If they've already killed her..." Ember's face twisted into a scowl. "I'll make them suffer."

A thundercrack rumbled over the landscape, despite the clear skies. Kali hissed.

"You're flooding yourself with Dark Energy, again. Stop it!"

Ember shook her head, feeling both foolish and afraid. "I'm sorry. I'm under a lot of stress, and Dark Magic senses that frustration. It's like a living thing, worming its way inside of you."

"I think it's already wormed its way inside of you," Kali said. "You've been, um, bellicose as of late, and Cedric said your eyes were glowing black when you confronted Chad Whitman."

Ember felt her heart skip a beat. "Oh no. Did anyone see?"

"Whitman sure as heck did," Kali said with a laugh. "Let's just say, Smothers had to mop under his chair after you left. Fortunately, your back was to the rest of the room, except..."

"Except what?" Ember swallowed hard. "Except for Reddy?"

"No, Hanky-Bob. Cedric thinks he may have seen."

Ember sighed. "We'll burn that bridge when we come to it. For now, I need your help casting some defensive wards."

"Wards strong enough to stop a bullet?" Kali's mental presence expressed trepidation. "That's dicey at best."

"We'll do the best we can."

Ember cast a spell which would stiffen the air around her body if anything fast moving entered her personal space, a kind of force field. She also enhanced her muscular and skeletal structure, rendering herself bullet resistant if not bullet proof.

Finally, she cast a spell which gave her the relative abilities of a forest toad. Her skin took on a bumpy, mottled appearance, and the fingers curled around her broomstick grew suction-cup-like appendages.

"There it is," Ember said, hovering a hundred feet in the air over Whitman's compound. "Do you see anything with your night vision?"

"Not a thing, except an old dog too feeble to scare the fleas off its back."

"I'm going down. Keep your eyes and ears peeled."

"Always."

Ember descended through the night air until she stepped onto the ground before the barn door. A formidable-looking padlock and chain barred her entry. She cast a spell which not only removed them, it did so silently. A purple energy field enveloped the padlock and chain, blocking in the clinking sounds as they unsnapped and unraveled.

The door creaked open, a loud sound which made Ember cringe. When no evil Whitman twins popped out of the woodwork, she relaxed a little and entered the pitch-black barn.

"Kathy?" Ember created a witch fire in her hand, lighting her way. She moved through the barn, past stacks of crates. On a whim, she lifted the tarp covering one, aghast to find C-4 explosives. The Foolkiller had plans. Big plans.

Ember heard a soft whimper from across the barn. She ran over to a horse stall and pushed it open.

Kathy looked up from the hay, practically cocooned in layers of hemp rope. Duct tape mummified the lower half of her face, holding in some kind of fat wadding. One of Kathy's eyes was swollen shut, drawing Ember's sympathy and ire.

"Kathy!" Ember swiftly fell to her knees beside her friend. The tricky knots angered her to the point she used a cantrip to undo them. "Are you okay?"

Kathy spat a rolled up sweat sock from her mouth and nodded. "I think so."

"Did he hit you?" Ember growled.

"No, I fell trying to escape," she said. "Listen, Ember, Chad Whitman has a twin brother!"

"I know, I know." Ember said. "Let's get you out of here."

Ember pulled Kathy to her feet and they exited the horse stall. They turned toward the entrance and froze in their tracks.

Blake Whitman stood there, one foot on top of a still, silent Kali while he aimed a shotgun their way.

"I don't know how you got in here," Blake said, his voice similar—but not quite the same—as his twin brother's. "But I know how you're going to leave. Feet first."

He squeezed the trigger, and fire blossomed from the twin barrels. Ember held her palm up and spoke a single, harsh arcane syllable. The flechettes from the shotgun hung suspended in the air.

Ember clenched her hand into a fist, and the shotgun shell fragments gathered into a jigsaw sphere of lead. She flicked the ball with her finger and it flew into Blake Whitman's jaw, knocking him out cold.

Roughly ten minutes later Cedric spun around the gravel road to find Ember and Kathy on Whitman's porch. Kathy held a mug of tea in her hands, a blanket draped over her shoulders. Kali sat on the fence near the gate button, flicking her tail as Cedric approached.

"Let me in, Kali," Cedric said.

"What's the Password?" Kali asked.

Cedric sighed. "I don't have time for this, Kali. Let me in."

"That's not the password."

"Just let him in, Kali," Ember said.

Kali pressed the button with her paw and the gate hummed as it slid open.

"Ruin my fun, will you?" Kali muttered.

"Where's Blake Whitman?" Cedric asked.

Ember grinned and pointed up. Whitman dangled by his ankles from tangled vines which Ember had summoned. He remained unconscious, a large bruise forming on his jaw.

"Guess I should have known you could handle yourself," Cedric said.

Ember grinned. "Well, I am a Sheriff's Deputy after all."

HOURS LATER, Ember, Cedric, and Kali drove back home. The day proved to be nice enough she could have her window rolled down. Ember inhaled deeply of the Louisiana air and sighed. Another case behind her. With the Foolkiller--both of them--safely behind bars, she could return to finding a way to restore Cedric's memories.

They pulled into the driveway at their home. Ash stood up from the porch swing and ran over to greet them, her face a mask of worry.

"Ash, what's wrong?" Ember asked. Her heart skipped a beat, and a cold fear gripped her belly. "Did something happen to April?"

"April's fine," Ash said swiftly. "Everybody's fine, it's just..."

"Just what?" Kali demanded.

Ash's jaw worked silently. "You'd better follow me."

Cedric and Ember exchanged glances before falling in line behind Ash. They marched up the porch steps and out to the garage.

Ember felt a tingle of magic in the air as they entered the garage. Her eyes widened when her gaze fell upon the broken window. Glass lay on the concrete floor, indicating it had been broken from the outside in.

"Did we get robbed?" Ember asked.

"I don't see anything missing," Cedric said. "All my tools are in place."

"I see something missing, all right!" Kali ran over to an empty spot on the shelf and sniffed carefully. Her nose wrinkled up and she sneezed. "Smells like swamp rot."

"What was on that shelf?" Cedric asked.

"The urn. The urn with you memories in it," Ash said. "It's been stolen."

Ember dropped to her knees, the pain barely registering at all compared to the despair welling in her heart.

Oh no...please, no...

Kali, Ash, and Cedric sought to comfort Ember as she broke down in heavy sobs.

TO BE CONTINUED...

TO KEEP up with sneak peeks and exclusive content, join my newsletter here: https://www.subscribepage.com/corrinewinters

PREVIEW

Check out my newest series, Hex and the City. This is a
fully built out world that I'm going for. Look for the Hex
and the City logo and you'll know you're in my world! If
you like funny paranormal chick lit cozy mystery, then
read on!

Witching & Moaning
Hex and the City, Book 1

By Corrine Winters

THIRTY-THREE

The yellow taxi's brakes squealed as it rolled to a stop outside the ten-story brownstone. Blair peered out of the back window, her heart leaping with joy inside her chest.

"There it is, Maeve." She turned her dark-tressed head to the side to grin at the young blonde woman on the seat beside her. "Isn't it great?"

Maeve pursed her lips as she leaned over Blair's lap to stare at the apartment building.

"It's so—so old!" Maeve gasped.

"It's New York City, Maeve. Everything is old." Blair gestured at the shallow steps leading up to the front entrance. "At least there's no crumbling masonry or passed out drunks on the stairwell."

Maeve opened her door, allowing a blast of crisp Autumn air inside the taxi. She glanced over at Blair and cocked an eyebrow. "*That's* our bar?"

Blair chuckled as she exited the taxi, the wind stirring her hair into her face. She moved it away from her eyes with a practiced flick of her finger and approached the taxi's open trunk. Maeve dragged her suitcases out and set them on the street while Blair slipped on a backpack.

"We were lucky to get a furnished apartment in Greenwich Village, Maeve." Blair looked up at the perfect azure sky between the rooftops overhead. "I mean, just look at this place. So much history, so much character! Everything is so big and sprawling. You could fit most of Middleton right here in this neighborhood."

"That's not saying much," Maeve grinned. "Don't get me wrong, I'm excited. I've just heard a lot of horror stories about rental properties in New York. Did you get everything?"

"Everything but Felix," Blair said. She reached into the back seat of the Taxi and carefully extracted a pet carrier. Blair peered through the mesh porthole at the curled-up bundle of white softness inside.

"It's no use being quiet, I'm already awake."

Blair chuckled. "Did you have a nice nap?"

"As nice a nap as one can have confined in a portable prison cell."

Blair unzipped the side of the carrier and Felix trotted out. He leaped adroitly up onto her shoulder and curled around her neck with a practiced familiarity.

"You know the taxi driver wouldn't let you in without a pet carrier."

"I know. I also know you could have cast a Suggestion spell and changed his mind—literally."

Maeve pursed her lips as she stood on the sidewalk nearby. "Um, Blair? People are staring?"

Blair shrugged. Several pedestrians and the Taxi driver himself eyed Blair with cautious suspicion.

"I'm sure in a city with more than eight million people, I'm not the only one talking to her pet kitty."

"Pet?" Felix sputtered. "*Pet?* I am a *familiar*. Calling me a pet is like calling a shark a big fish."

"I'm sorry, Felix," Blair said, scratching him behind his ear.

"No! Stop it! I want to be angry—" Felix's eyes closed, and he leaned into Blair's scratching fingernail. "Ooooh yeah, that's the spot."

They entered the building, luggage wheels bouncing up the steps. A black cat looked up at Felix from atop a garbage can with curious eyes.

"Hey, watch yourself," Felix hissed. "This is MY street now."

"Felix, behave."

"You've got to set the record straight with the big city cats. Otherwise, they think they can just walk all over you."

The building's interior enveloped them in the smell of Murphy's wood polish and a sickly sweet aroma Blair couldn't place. To the left of the entrance sat a small, caged-in security office. A balding, heavyset man with a pencil thin mustache and a sleeveless shirt which displayed how muscular his arms weren't stood up swiftly. Blair noted the Swisher Sweets butts crushed into the nearby ashtray, the likely source of the pungent smell.

"Hello, ladies," he said in a husky voice while he looked them up and down with what he no doubt thought were bedroom eyes. "You must be my new tenants. The Barrow sisters?"

Blair forced a smile onto her face, even though the man creeped her out on almost every level.

"Yes, we are. I'm Blair, and this is my sister Maeve."

Maeve's smile displayed more strain than Blair's own. Felix's ears went back as he regarded the man.

"I'm Gary, your building super and property manager." He opened a drawer under his desk and rummaged around. "Let's see...here we go. Fourth floor, corner apartment."

He withdrew old-looking brass keys with a rattle and laid them on the desk. Instead of sliding the keys through the security hole at the bottom of this mesh cage, however, Gary cocked his head to the side.

"Sisters, huh?" He leered at each of them in turn. "Was your dad by any chance a traveling salesman?"

Maeve put her hands on her hips. "What's that supposed to mean?"

"Nothing, nothing, I'm sure blondes and brunettes crop up in the same family all the time." He slid the keys to Blair's waiting grasp. "You have any problems with your apartment, maintenance issues, or you just want to talk... just let old Gary know. I'll take extra good care of you."

"Thanks," Blair said, baring her teeth in what she hoped was a smile and not a grimace. The sisters gathered their luggage and strode to the elevator.

"What a creepo," Felix said. "Want me to cough up a hairball in his underwear drawer?"

"You'll do no such thing, Felix," Blair said. "We're new here. We aren't in the Midwest anymore."

"I think this is our apartment," Maeve said, pointing at the paint-chipped but sturdy-seeming door.

"You want to do the honors?" Blair asked, holding up the jangling keys for Maeve.

"Wow," Maeve said as she took the keys in her hands. "This is really happening, isn't it?"

Maeve turned the key, undoing the deadbolt first, then

the lock on the spindle. She pushed the door open with some difficulty until it shuddered into the apartment. Sunlight spilled in through a large bay window, pigeons cooing outside on the concrete edifice. Polished hardwood floors cast the window's reflection in blurry, upside down effigy. Blair sighed in relief.

"No mildew smell, that's good."

"Yeah, it's surprisingly clean," Maeve said. "Just, um...small."

"It's New York City, Maeve. This is a palace compared to some places we looked at." Blair turned her gaze about, taking in the open concept kitchen/living space, the doors on either side of the apartment which likely led to the two bedrooms. The black skeleton of a fire escape hung outside the window.

"How thoughtful of them to put in an entrance stairway just for cats," Felix quipped.

Maeve went to the wall and flipped the switch, but neither the ceiling fan nor its attached lighting array stirred.

"Oh no," Maeve said. "It's busted."

"I guess we better tell Gary," Blair said with open distaste.

Maeve cocked an angular golden eyebrow. "Are you sure there's not some other way you can handle this?"

Blair nodded. "Yes. I'd rather not give Gary an excuse to come up here."

She laid her hand against the smoothly painted drywall and let her senses shift from the mundane realm into the Arcane. Her Electromancy talent let her sense the currents and wires moving through the walls and ceiling.

Blair sent a pulse of her innate Eldritch power pulsing through the outlet, and found the problem; a short in the wires some four feet from the switch.

"It's not the whole apartment, just this switch," Blair announced, sparks crackling in her eyes.

"That's good news," Maeve replied. "Can you fix it?"

"Yes, it's a simple application of Transmutation magic to mend the wires back together."

Felix twitched his tail. "You better let me back you up. You know Transmutation isn't your strongest Discipline of magic."

Maeve chuckled softly. "For a self-taught witch, Felix, I think she's pretty darn impressive."

"I'm not self-taught," Blair said with a frown. "My bio-mother's Grimoire had lots of notes. I almost think she was trying to prepare for...well, you know."

Felix brushed his cheek against Blair's ankle in a show of solidarity. "We gonna cast this cantrip or what?"

Blair nodded. She linked her mind, her essence with Felix's. As usual, his thoughts leaped out at her like flashes of synaptic lightning. The brightest pulse of all bore the words and somatic gestures of her mending cantrip.

Blair held her hands out to the sides, then brought them together slowly as she muttered the words of power under her breath. When her hands met before her sternum, fingers entwined, she finished the incantation and sent her intentions into the metaphysical realm of magic.

Three of the lights flicked into sudden brightness, and the fan swished into life.

"See?" Felix purred as he rubbed against Blair's calf. "Thanks to my help, the spell went off without a hitch. You sure were lucky when I showed up to serve as your familiar."

Maeve and Blair chuckled.

"Your modesty is underwhelming, Felix," Maeve said.

"I'm a cat. If you want modesty, you're looking in the wrong place."

Blair chuckled as she extracted her phone and looked at the screen. A gasp escaped her lips when she saw the time.

"I've got to get going. Don't want to be late for my first day of work!"

THIRTY-FOUR

Blair stepped out of her bedroom, a look of distaste on her face as she gestured broadly at herself.

"How do I look?"

Maeve pursed her lips. "Good..."

"You look like the love child of Hillary Clinton and Tilda Swinton cosplaying as Elaine from *Seinfeld*."

Maeve gaped at Felix in shock. "That wasn't nice!"

Blair sighed, looking at the plain gray skirt suit adorning her lithe form. "This isn't my style, but I'm trying to look professional."

"What does it matter how you dress if you're a writer?" Felix asked, his tail twitching in annoyance. "Come on, your fine feline familiar shall once again save the day by picking out a better outfit."

"No time, Felix," Blair said, checking her phone. "I've got to get going.

She glanced over at Maeve. "When do classes start?"

"Next Monday, why?"

"You should stop by the University and pick up your schedule."

"Already downloaded it," Maeve said with a wink. "Knock 'em dead."

"Not literally, of course," Felix called as Blair headed out the door. "Unless it's an Atragon Demon in disguise."

Blair squinted at her phone as she closed the door behind her, calculating the fastest trajectory to TheShoot.com's office. According to the map, she could shave off five minutes of her walk by exiting the apartment building through the rear.

Blair exited the elevator on the second floor, where the rear exit was located. Reservations prickled her mind as she walked down the worn hallway, past gutted apartments still under renovation. It didn't seem to be the most inviting path out of the building.

She pushed open the heavy rear door and found herself at the top of a two-tiered wooden stairway, obviously a recent edition which didn't match the other architecture. Blair thumped down the steps, growing aware of harsh voices speaking from under the stairwell.

"Hey, if you'll just tell Maroni to give me another week, two tops, I'll have it all turned around, I swear."

Blair's eyes narrowed at the sound of Gary's pleading voice.

"Gary, we gave you an extension already. You know the drill. We've got to set an example."

"Yeah, Gary. We know you've got to work on the building and stuff, so we're not going to break nothing. You might be peeing blood for a while, though."

Blair peered through the timbers of the stairwell, seeing two men pinning Gary up against the brownstone. While she wasn't exactly friends with Gary, Blair's upbringing and conscience wouldn't allow her to just walk away.

She summoned up her eldritch power, augmented by a

ley line overhead—one of the reasons she'd wanted to live in the Village was because of that ley line, a power source for witches and warlocks. To the mundane folk on the street, it was invisible. To her it pulsed and throbbed with a light akin to the aurora borealis, even in broad daylight.

Blair muttered the words to a Glamour, weaving the incantation together with some difficulty. Without Felix to help focus her mind, Blair struggled as she wove the spell.

In the end, her Glamour didn't quite come off without a hitch. A cop car pulled into the rear lot of the apartment building, the two officers inside staring intently at the scene under the stairwell. However, the illusion was visual only. The car's engine made no sound, and if the thugs threatening Gary had taken the time to inspect it carefully, they'd have found other flaws.

The cop car lacked an exhaust pipe, and instead of saying NYPD on the side it read Middleton Police Department. Fortunately, the thugs were mundane and had never encountered illusion magic before.

"This ain't over, Gary." The men released him and strode swiftly up the stairs. They frowned at Blair as they moved up past her, but she was careful to act studiously oblivious.

Blair walked out into the street and let the illusion dissipate. She checked her phone and found her magical stunt hadn't cost her as much time as she'd thought.

She walked to the building where TheShoot.com rented office space. Unlike the apartment brownstone she shared with Maeve, the office building had seen better days. Blair noted the elevator was out of order and walked the six stories to her new office.

The frosted glass door leading to TheShoot.com was easy to find, thanks to the logo painted on the smooth surface. Blair opened the door and peered anxiously inside, finding twin rows of cubicles with people furiously typing away in all but one of them.

Blair entered the office and glanced about until she saw a door with the word 'management' emblazoned across its surface with big black letters. She made for it, walking swiftly over the thin carpet and reaching out to grasp the doorknob.

"Oh, hey, are you Blair?"

Blair turned about to find a small, brown skinned woman with frizzy red hair excitedly approaching. Her infectious smile quickly spread to Blair's face.

"Yes, I am. Blair Barrows."

"Jessica Forrester." The woman pumped her hand enthusiastically. "I'm so glad to meet you. Our office manager Delia is going to be out until late this afternoon, so she asked me to get you oriented."

"Thanks."

Blair followed Jessica to the empty cubicle. A dusty monitor and tower set up awaited her, complete with a sticker denoting the username and password for access.

"So, are you familiar with TheShoot.com?"

Blair frowned. "A little? It's come up on my news feed before."

Jessica snorted. "Yeah, well, I wouldn't call us a news site. Anyway, I'll show you how to log onto your company email. That's where you get your assignments every day. If you can't do at least six articles a day, you get a warning. Then you get written up and fired."

"Wow, okay," Blair said. "I'll do my best."

"You'll do fine," Jessica said. "Pardon me for asking, but you're not from the City, are you?"

"No," Blair felt a tinge of color and warmth come to her cheeks. "Is it that obvious?"

"To me it is. You seem too sweet and nice to be a New York native. Don't worry, stick with me and I'll have you kicking butt and taking names in no time."

"Thanks, Jessica," Blair smiled. If her boss were as friendly and helpful as Jessica, TheShoot.com might turn out to be a nice place to work after all.

Until she opened her email and saw the articles on her itinerary. She was disheartened to realize that she was going to be writing little more than vapid clickbait articles.

"Top ten Hollywood Hotties?" she muttered, staring at her screen. "The Summer's Most Coked Out Celebs? Seven things in your house right now that can kill you?"

"Told you," Jessica said from the next cubicle over.

Blair worked on her 'articles' for the rest of the afternoon. At four o'clock sharp, her fellow cubicle denizens began packing up to head home.

"Um, did the manager ever come back?" Blair asked Jessica.

"No, but don't worry. When you log in for your assignments you essentially clock in. Delia's not the most softly spoken of leaders, but she's pretty good when it comes to payroll."

Jessica and Blair walked down the steps to the street together, Jessica chatting up a storm.

"Have you ever done yoga? Danielle and I do yoga three times a week, you should join us sometime. I think you'd like her; she wants to be a big time journalist like you. How long have you been in the city? No kidding, just moved today? This is kismet. We're going to be the best of friends, you and I. Plus, you're really cute. All the guys will flock over you, and I'll get all your cast offs. Don't look at me like that, you're in New York now, sweetie. Time to enjoy life!"

Despite the non-stop barrage of speech, Blair decided she liked Jessica by the time they reached the bottom level. She was...sunny.

"Say, do you want to get a latte? There's a neat little coffee shop down the street, hole in the wall really, but they've got the best biscotti."

"Thanks, but my sister is waiting on me," Blair said. "And if I don't get home and give my cat some tuna, there's going to be a devil to pay."

"Aww, you've got a kitty? I'd love to see him sometime."

Blair noted the implied request and smiled. "Sure, that would be great."

"Awesome sauce! See you tomorrow, Blair."

Blair felt a strange mix of emotions. Contentment that she'd completed her first day of work, joy at having achieved her dream of moving to New York City, and that strange feeling of disconnect which goes hand in hand with being in a new place.

She came around the last corner before home and saw flashing emergency vehicle lights.

Did I forget to banish my illusion spell?

Blair quickly realized the police cars, ambulance, and coroner's wagon were all quite real...and parked directly behind her building.

Her mouth gaped open when she saw the body bag being loaded onto a gurney. Someone had died...

"Excuse me, are you Blair Barrows?"

Blair turned about to see a tall, dark-haired man wearing a frumpy suit and somber expression which diminished his otherwise handsome features. She noted one of his ears had a slight fold, and he had the walk—and build—of an athlete.

"Yes, I am."

The man flashed a shiny badge at her. "Detective Christopher Farrow, NYPD. Do you have a sister named Maeve?"

Blair's knees grew weak. She looked over at the body bag as it was loaded onto the coroner's black wagon.

Oh no...Maeve...

Read more here!